# FUBAR: BLACKOUT

HARRY CARPENTER

*First published by Midnight Destiny Publishing 2020*



*First edition*
*ISBN: 978-0-578-55540-9*

*Dedicated to the men and women I served with while in the United States Army. You guys are my family, and my best memories lie with our adventures. Stay safe, Hooah.*
*To SPC Stan Soko, and SSG Jimmy Carpenter, most importantly.*

*To my wife, you are probably what keeps most of the nightmares and crazy thoughts at bay.*

*"Whoever said the pen is mightier than the sword obviously never encountered automatic weapons."*

**-Douglas MacArthur**

# Preface

As I mounted the m249 machine gun against my shoulder, I felt the weight of the entire weapon. I had never really had the opportunity to fire one of these bad boys before, but by god, there was a first for everything. I flipped the safety selector switch, removing the weapon from safe. I closed my eyes for a brief moment, knowing time was of the essence. I reopened them, steadied my breathing as I squeezed softly on the trigger. I fired small round bursts into the crowd of these things. I barely knew how to work one of these because my military career thus far has been magazine-fed weapons. I prayed to whoever was listening for the belt to remain free with no snag. I continued to three to five-round burst my way to the base exchange. The good news: these things were going down with regular ammo. The bad news: I don't know if I have enough ammo for all of them.

# Acknowledgment

I'd like to thank the following for their inspiration and collaboration on this idea. Your characters will live on, and may they be the bad-ass you wished you were. (I kid)

Brian, Eladio, Cait, David, JP, Jim, Nelson, Mike, Rico, and numerous others that I may have forgotten.

Thanks for your personalities, likenesses, and attitudes to bring the characters to life!

# Chapter 1

*FOB Centurion, IZ*
*1300 Local*
*February 10, 2010*

It was hot. Why was it so damn hot? I removed some of the Velcro that held together my IBA to let some air in. These vests were always so stuffy and tight. It was February, a few days before Valentine's Day and I was sweating like a hog. Don't even get me started on the sand. At the end of every mission, I'd find sand in places that it never should be able to reach. Given its illusiveness, I'm sure there is some sand in my taint currently forming a pearl as we speak.

This dump wasn't all that bad though, we did have our lovely field rations to keep morale high. The usual MRE assortment consisted of bland meals. In addition to the poorly heated meals, there was the highly coveted Jalapeno cheese spread, and stale gum to top off the delicacy. We had just finished eating our meals when our squad leader, Sergeant Matthews, signaled to round up. I tossed my chili mac into the empty packaging, stood up from my position, slinging the M4 assault rifle over my shoulder. I began to make my way over to the group, stomping through mounds of Iraqi sand as I did.

"Well done, crew. Top was pleased with this exercise, and your progress today. I've taken shits that were more impressive, but if he's happy, I'm happy. Let's get ready to pack it in and roll out," ordered Sergeant Matthews.

Matthews was a decent size guy, not too muscular but by no means out of shape. He was always a fitness star. He loved to show off how many push-ups he could crank out at the required physical training test. One hundred and thirty-four was his record. And he only stopped there because he got bored. Personally, I envied him. I was lucky if I could muster up the passing grade for push-ups. I was always a runner. Cardio was my game, and I was damn proud of it. I always figured if I needed to, running would get me out of danger a hell of a lot quicker than dropping to the floor and pushing my body up repeatedly.

We packed up the training site as quickly as anyone could. We weren't super-soldiers, nor did we claim to be. We spent the day at a gauntlet of qualification ranges trying to shoot little paper men. I always figured, given the situation, if we were attacked by paper targets, I'd be a hero. We tore down our targets and boxed the fresh ones into the plastic tough-boxes, loading them into the back of the canvas top Humvee. We used an unarmored vehicle because, frankly, we weren't in any real danger. This was a calm territory compared to the others, save for a rocket incoming now and then.

There was so much expended brass left over. For a couple of desk jockeys, we sure as hell used a ton of ammo. The downside is that we all never shot perfect accuracy. While inaccurate, we could lay down a hell of a lot of suppressive fire if we needed to. I wasn't half bad with a weapon if I do say so myself. My grouping was always pretty close, and once I was dialed in for windage, the targets didn't stand a chance. SGT Matthews always hated how I fired at the targets. I'd still justify that the target would not be happy and want to continue fighting afterward. Out of my fifteen rounds, five in the chest, three in the groin, two in the leg. The remaining rounds would hit the hands and ears of the target. I personally would throw my weapon down if I were shot in the ear.

After we policed up all of the expended brass casings and returned the range to its empty state, we began to load into the vehicles. There were only four of us in this squad; Sergeant Matthews headed the pack. I considered myself a bit of a rebel, going against the grain as often as I could. I was smoked more often than I should have been, but I have no regrets. All that really did was enhance my push-up ability in the long run. Then there was PFC Alexopoulos. She wore her hair tight like the boys, and she was short. Make no mistake: she was an absolute badass. We called her 'X' for short. X was always playing pranks on everyone. She enjoyed horsing around with the boys and could honestly hold her own when it came to physicality. Let's just say I wouldn't dare go against her in a combatives contest. Lastly, there was Specialist Martinez. This guy was a fitness beast as well. Bald headed, with a New York hometown love, Spanish passion and attitude to match. He had some crazy arm tats that ran the length of his arms. I don't think I'd have the guts to get a sleeve done, let alone a single tattoo. I have an irrational fear of needles.

We loaded into the Humvee, which we named Dancer. We had several vehicles we named after Santa's reindeer. You have to make things fun where you can. SGT Matthews insisted on being the driver because it was one of the few connections he had to the world back home. I personally didn't mind riding shotgun as his second in command. As a team leader, I enjoyed a few perks, such as riding in the passenger seat by default. We were headed to get some chow. I was pretty glad it was lunchtime because I was starving. SGT Matthews drove us down the long winding dirt road that led back to our living quarters and parked the vehicle at our headquarters.

We walked down the footpath that led to the dining facility. It was a big white tent-like building in the middle of the base. It wasn't a sturdy building or permanent structure by any means, but it did the job. We walked in, flashed our ID cards, and grabbed our trays. We all made our way to our food preferences. SGT Matthews lived for stir-fry. X always ate the meatiest meats that could be found. If there was a steak, it was on her plate. Martinez ate healthily. He was a green and low-fat kind of guy. Me? Put me in front of the breakfast food any day. I would grab an omelet any day that they were available, and thankfully, they were served all day long.

We began to eat, not making much small talk as we did. We kept to ourselves mainly, but there were some soldiers in our unit we befriended. SPC Eriks came to sit with us this day. He was always loud-mouthed, but well mannered. He reminded me of Jack Black a bit. He could almost pass as an illegitimate son of his if I hadn't seen Eriks' actual father before deployment. Eriks sat across from SGT Matthews. He never sat with his own squad for some reason, and Matthews could sense that. He took him in as an "adopted soldier" when he wasn't working. He was an honorary team member.

The omelet was life-changing as always. Ham, eggs, and cheese wrapped into one delicious meal. X was already done her food by the time I was halfway into my breakfast feast. I had no idea how someone could digest that much red meat so quickly, but who was I to judge. The dining facility, or the DFAC as it was commonly referred to, was a giant room, full of buffet-style food, and picnic-like tables. For being a shoddy tent, the interior was worth enjoying. As always, before throwing our food away, I grabbed several soda cans from the coolers and stashed them in my various cargo pockets. I wanted to be healthy, but damn, soda was delicious.

We sat outside and waited for a bit while Martinez smoked a cigarette. It was his only vice and was otherwise considered the healthiest dude I knew. There wasn't much to do when deployed. You either worked out, got fat, or took up a vice, like chewing tobacco or smoking. I never really saw Martinez smoke back home.

"Not bad shooting today. What's on the agenda for tomorrow, sarge?" Martinez called out to SGT Matthews, in between puffs of his cigarette.

"Tomorrow? I'm not sure. I gotta find a way to keep us busy. I'm open for suggestions," he replied, shrugging his shoulders as he did.

I rested against one of the concrete barricades. These barriers were all over the place. They were in place mainly to deter someone from driving a vehicle through a building, and you could tell by the placement.

"Can we see if the chief has anything going on? Maybe we can squeeze our way into one of her taskings?" I asked.

I really enjoyed working under our chief warrant officer. She always tasked us with fun things and loved working with us. She was a kind soul as well, not very militant. The exact opposite of what the Army tends to make you into.

"Cool. I'll check with Chief Hill later today after I drop you assclowns off at your CHU," he said as he moved toward the Humvee.

Martinez finished his smoke, and we all headed over toward the vehicle. Dancer was the greatest thing our little squad ever commandeered. It came with our primary tactical vehicle, and that one remained stationary. Dancer was what made things so much better. The drawback it presented was that it frequently overheated, and we were about to be reminded of how much we hated that aspect.

"Son of a bitch nuts!" SGT Matthews cried out, and he kicked the tire of Dancer.

The engine frequently overheated. It was partly due to shoddy craftsmanship, and partly due to the damn weather we had in this country. It was always too damn hot. We took care of the vehicle in the only way we could: we poured water on the engine to cool it down. Now I know, every car guy in the world just cringed knowing what we did. But we did it and damned if it didn't work every time. Dancer started back up just fine, and we hit the road to "The Village" as the housing area was doubly named.

Matthews parked the vehicle outside of the entrance to The Village. We couldn't take vehicles down there, so we walked from here. Luckily, the rows of storage trailers turned housing weren't hard to traverse. The Hesco barricades make a maze of the area, but it wasn't too hard to get through. We parted ways, only to reconvene once again for our night-shift operations the next day. It was great to put a long day behind all of us.

# Chapter 2

*FOB Centurion, IZ*
*2200 Local*
*February 10, 2010*

I was woken abruptly by loud noises outside of my room. My compartmentalized housing unit, or CHU, was a two-person shipping container that held our personal possessions. I had the windows blocked out because I would be asleep during the day. That was the downside to the night shift, I suppose. I reached over to my clothing bag and pulled out my cleanest pair of ACU pants and pulled them on. I tossed a tan undershirt on and laced my boots. The noise happened again. *What was happening out there?*

I unlocked and thrust open the door, rifle in hand. The Army always trained you to never leave your weapon behind. My eyes adjusted to the night sky, trying to make out what was happening. I could see shapes in the distance. PFC's Dalog and Studds came running by my door.

"Man, you won't believe how many rockets these guys have!" Studds laughed as he pointed to another incoming rocket.

Of course. Incoming fire and the incoming alarm didn't go off. I grabbed my vest and followed the other two toward the concrete barricade at the end of our row. We could duck in there and hope for the best. If there was a direct hit, we were goners, but it did the job protecting from shrapnel. We huddled up, waiting for the all-clear. Studds, Dalog and I were the only ones to take up residency in this particular barrier.

Dalog and Studds were also in my unit. They worked in a different section, but we were no strangers to each other. Dalog worked across the base, doing some hush-hush level work. I honestly didn't know what he did. It could have been an act, and they really didn't do anything but play cards all day, or maybe he had that Area 51 level access. Studds, on the other hand, I knew exactly what he did. He lived in the gym. He took supplements, protein, and just about anything else he could do to pump himself up.

The whistle of the rockets overhead began to taper off. The explosions stopped altogether. Thank god, because honestly, I had things to do. The intercom blared out an all-clear signal, and business resumed. We split ways, returning to our respective rooms. I changed into my fitness uniform; a t-shirt and black shorts. I made my way to the showers to get clean and prepare for the work shift. I hated the showers when I was in training, but the ones in combat were not half bad. They were private, and you even had a shower door. I think the worst thing I hated was the circular showers, and several dudes faced each other. At least facing a wall offered some modesty.

I cleaned the pertinent parts and changed into my uniform once I returned to my room. I knew SGT Matthews would be around soon with the Humvee and I had to hustle. Maybe he was delayed by the rockets, and I had a few extra minutes? I collected my IBA, helmet, and weapon and donned each individual piece of gear. You never knew when something would go down, as they say. I walked out, heading toward the end of the row where Matthews would always park Dancer. I saw our Humvee parked, but SGT Matthews was nowhere to be found. I called his name out a few times, but I got no reply. I decided to wait for the others before causing any sort of alarm for our unattended vehicle.

I must have been sitting there for ten minutes or so before X showed up. She seemed to drag a bit as if she didn't sleep well. She grumpily tossed her bag into the back of the vehicle and threw herself into the back seat. She didn't close the door, but it was evident she didn't want to be bothered. I dared not speak a word either. I continued to sit on the hood of Dancer and waited. Over the horizon rounding the corner, I spotted SGT Matthews walking with Martinez in tow. Great, the gang is all here.

No one really said anything. We greeted each other with generic grunts and nods and boarded the vehicle. We drove over to the DFAC to eat our food because it was dinner time. This meant it was our breakfast. Today was Stir-Fry Wednesday. A real missed opportunity to push that at least two more days. But it was SGT Matthews' favorite day. It was like a damn national holiday to him. Frankly, I've never seen someone put away that many noodles before in my life. We parked alongside the concrete Jersey barriers that lined the outside of the building and went inside. I opted for my usual breakfast collection of bacon, eggs, and more bacon. I like to diversify sometimes.

Our usual seat was free as one by one we gathered the food to eat and settled in. Nobody was saying a word, just hunkering down over their food plates and eating. I decided I'd break the silence.

"Who shit in everyone's oatmeal this evening?" I asked, jokingly laughing as I delivered the words.

X was the first one to look up. She appeared offended but was oddly enough the first to speak up.

"For the record I hate oatmeal. And I didn't sleep much with those a-holes firing their stupid rockets at us all night. Sorry if I'm grumpy. I have coffee and an energy drink now, I'll be better in a few," she said as she popped the top to the small Rip-It energy drink they supplied us within Iraq. Those things were awful, but when they're free, they're free. I can't complain too much. I hated coffee, so this was my alternative.

SGT Matthews finished his first tray full of stir-fry. He moved onto the to-go plate he requested. He never took food out of the DFAC, he just liked stir-fry that much. Who was I, or anyone else for that matter, to stop him? Martinez sat back from the table after finishing his massive plate of food.

"Jesus Christ if I eat any more, Holmes, I'll explode," Martinez bellowed as he rubbed his stomach, letting out a loud disgusting belch to follow.

"For dick's sake, Martinez. Can you show any manners or respect? Ladies are present. Can you apologize for being a revolting disgusting human being?" SGT Matthews barked at Martinez, his hand extended with all fingers pointing at Martinez. Knife-hand as we liked to call it.

Martinez looked behind him at the few Air Force guys that were seated behind us. He made it obvious enough to get their attention.

"Sorry for being rude, ladies," he said, being an absolute smartass with a massive smile on his face.

The Air Force guys didn't say a word. They just kept eating. Maybe they're just used to the abuse from soldiers and Marines. After a while, you grow numb to the ribbing and jabbing from the different branches. Martinez was always an asshole, but he was the right kind of an asshole. He was the guy who would set a dislocated shoulder while making fun of your arm at the same time. I was never sure if it was a good thing or a bad thing. I'll assume good, for his sake.

PFC X put her head in her hands. She clearly didn't want to be at work tonight. I don't blame her because I felt the same way. The rocket attack didn't do anyone any favors. They were always so frequent, you'd think we would be used to it by now. This was a regularly scheduled system: wake up, rockets. Eat, rockets. Practically anything you could think of was typically followed up by a rocket attack. It was almost comforting to know they were on a routine out here.

SGT Matthews stood up from the table slowly and made his way to drop off his trash. We each followed behind slowly. None of us really felt like being awake for this shift. Something about last night's rocket barrage was different than the others. It was longer than any other attack on the base. We didn't hear any chatter of destroyed buildings or the Explosive Ordinance Division having to take care of unexploded rockets. Usually, that was the first thing on the lips of every chatty Kathy in the dining hall.

"Let's roll," SGT Matthews called out, as he started toward the Humvee.

Tonight, we didn't bother to wait for SPC Martinez to light up his usual post-meal smoke. He climbed into the rear passenger seat and didn't say a word. This was highly unusual, even for him. Remember how I said that this night just didn't feel right? I was correct in my assumption. Once we arrived at the headquarters building, we unloaded from the Humvee and headed inside.

The building was an old concrete bunker. It may have been a warehouse or something at one point in time, but for now, it was a hollow shell of its former self. It now housed a few offices, desks, chairs and what felt like a lifetime supply of Girl Scout cookies. Those things were addictive, and a soldiers best and worst friend. I followed SGT Matthews to the office that we shared and set my belongings down. I usually traveled with my personal laptop and a hard drive full of movies and television programs.

PFC X headed over to her office across the hall. And when I say office, I use the term lightly. Don't picture a perfect little hallway, tightly knit cubicles, and an office atmosphere. Picture instead a concrete

warehouse, with plywood walls that reached only halfway to the ceiling, and makeshift lighting hung from parachute cords. The desks, however, were actual desks. The floor was concrete. It wasn't too bad to be working our shift at headquarters. We dismissed the previous team and said our farewells. We were in charge of the show for the next twelve or so hours.

Martinez apparently decided to go for that smoke after all. He remained outside and didn't join us for some time. Martinez came in through the giant steel doors that separated us from the harsh world outside. The whole time he walked down the ramp to join us, he looked over his shoulder. I only noticed this because I was rooting through the latest shipment of cookies and finding my favorites.

"You good bro?" I called out to Martinez, stuffing a peanut butter cookie in my face.

"Yeah, I just feel weird, ya know? Like, something ain't right," Martinez said, reaching out for one of my cookies. "You feel it too, right?"

I nodded.

"Yo, Sarge! You check the network for any issues? We got any updates? Nothing got blowed up last night?" joked Martinez.

SGT Matthews grunted from his office. We weren't sure if that was a grunt of confirmation or not. The two of us decided silently to go into the office and see. He was looking through an assortment of emails and other updates on our alert system. There was nothing about any strikes on the base.

SGT Matthews leaned back. "Yeah, there ain't nothing. Stupid morons missed us entirely. They must be getting dumber over time," He turned his monitor around for us to see as he told us.

Martinez glanced at it. He shrugged and went off to begin his nightly tasks. Communications. Phone calls and radio were his things. He was decent at it, despite his accent. He could articulate clearly over the radio. Hell, he sounded better than I did. I could barely remember the phonetic alphabet and looked like a jackhole every time I called out a spelling. It wasn't uncommon to hear me say "Oswald, Monkey," In place of Oscar Mike. Unlike me, he had a voice for the radio.

Martinez took his post and sat by the radio. He pulled out a book to read while he rested. A smutty romance novel, oddly enough. This one was about some cowboy who fell in love with a farmhand or something, and they banged like rabbits every three pages. This was also the plot of literally every single romance book he read, now that I think about it. I don't know why he read them, but man was he into them. He would put his feet up on the table and kick back and lose himself.

X would always slip away alone into her office. She worked the supply room for the night shift and loved every second of it. X got her own office and could order things within reason without question. I think she's the only one of us with a chin-up bar in their room. It wasn't an abuse of power, because honestly, our higher-ups saw it as a vital step toward physical fitness. They ate that crap up like it was candy.

I fired up my laptop and set it on the desk. I decided to wander around while it loaded up. I hated computers, but I don't know how the soldiers before me survived with writing paper letters to their family and sharing stories with each other. A few months into this deployment, and I gained a newfound respect for the struggle. I picked up my rifle from the rifle rack by the office door and withdrew my patrol cap from my pocket. I motioned to SGT Matthews I was going to walk around for a second, and he nodded in acknowledgment.

The night air was still. This was what I loved about working the night shift, the stillness. There was no brass walking around giving you orders, saluting, yelling. Nothingness. It was beautiful. This was my routine each night. I would take a stroll out in the late-night and just think. Sometimes I'd take my rifle, sometimes I didn't. No one was outside to correct me, and frankly, we weren't in that much danger of being overrun to really be a concern in the front of my brain. Tonight, I grabbed it and regretted taking it.

I went for a walk around the familiar roads that surrounded the headquarters building and surrounding structures. I must have walked for a quarter mile when I decided to pocket my patrol cap again. I unzipped my ACU top and felt the cool, crisp breeze pierce through the tan undershirt. *Freedom*, I thought. This was liberating, and the highlight of my shift. I'd typically wander the same path for about an hour, and make my way back in. The moonlight and sporadic street light being the only illumination I had. This was much better than cooking in the hot sun during the day.

It must have been around two in the morning by the time I pulled an about-face and started walking back toward the headquarters building. Something still felt odd about tonight though. I couldn't put my finger on it. For starters, no one was lobbing rockets in our direction. I took that as a blessing. Maybe it was a holiday these people celebrated, and I just forgot, who knows? I rounded the corner nearest the perimeter of the base. The worst case for me is that the guy in the high tower looks down and yells at me for half-assing the uniform, but chances are he

won't care enough to bother. I continued my trip down the dirt path.

The road I took back had a lot fewer street lights. Moonlight was the only thing I used to guide me, and thanks to my night vision, I could see pretty well in the dark. My eyes typically did adjust well to dim lighting, something I was always proud of. I could almost make out colors in a dark room at times. It moved. I didn't quite make out what *it* was, but I'd be damned if it didn't move. I blinked a few times and tried to look harder. There was something in the shadows that moved. I decided I should zip up my top and throw the hat on. I'd hate to be demoted for not wearing my headgear.

I didn't yell out to them because it was still late at night. I didn't want to risk waking someone important up, and I also didn't want to blurt out a giant "you are here" to my position. I decided I would just casually try to stroll by and not make eye contact unless necessary. Us night shifters had the same mentality I figured: Don't talk to me, and I won't talk to you. I quickened my pace and continued down the road. The other guy didn't budge. They just stood there in the distance.

Maybe I'm just seeing someone that isn't there?

I pushed forward down the path some more. I was almost at a light jog. Part of me wanted to see who the hell was standing there, and part of me really just wanted to get back to the headquarters. As I drew closer, this guy just ran to the right, toward the perimeter wall! Who runs toward the wall? In one move, he skittered up and over the wall, disappearing into the night sky. Who was this guy? Was this a guy? It couldn't be people. People don't skitter. Right?

I began to doubt myself as I quickened my pace even more to a slow run. I hurried past a lot of the dark areas that were not well lit and rounded several corners to make my way back to the headquarters offices. I pushed through the large steel doors and closed them behind me. Part of me wanted to make the cliché move and lock and barricade due to what I saw, but I didn't even know what I saw.

I went into the office with SGT Matthews, who was in the middle of watching some Japanese Anime movie. He took out an earbud as if he knew I wanted to say something. I'm guessing it was drawn on my face. I didn't even know what to say to him. How do you tell another grown man that you just saw a person scuttle over the wall? That statement also sounded stupid, but I took a deep breath and began.

"Ok, so I was out for my walk, and something happened." I started.

Matthews took out the second earbud and gave me full attention. X even came out of her office, concerned with how hard I slammed the door.

"This is crazy. I'm not crazy, but this sounds crazy. Ok, so- "

"What? What is it?" Martinez called across the building, interrupting my story.

"I was getting there. Anyway, I was walking around my usual walk. The weather was great, and a perfect night to be honest. They haven't even rocketed us yet. Anyway, I was out near the Stryker lot, and I

noticed someone, or something, that freaked me out."

"How did it freak you out?" SGT Matthews asked, his expression showing he was done with the story before it began.

"Well, I thought I saw someone. I put my uniform back together, and – "

"Why was your uniform not together? Didn't we talk about keeping your cap and top to standard?"

"Yeah, but I did that, and I got closer to this dude. Turns out, it wasn't a dude? They crawled over the perimeter and out to the city," I said, sitting against the edge of my desk.

SGT Matthews sat forward in his chair. He put his hands together and placed his fingertips to his lips, as if in deep thought.

"So, you're saying someone was outside and climbed the wall?" He asked.

"No, not like crawled with hands and feet. Like a damn bug or something," I responded, trying to be clear with what I saw, even though I still wasn't sure what I saw.

He smiled. I wasn't being taken seriously. I've seen enough movies while downrange in this country to know how this plays out. I'll be the first one eaten by the killer. The moth man is going to get me, or whatever it is outside the walls. I had to be firm.

"No, you're not hearing me out. Come with me and take a look."

I couldn't believe the words came out of my mouth. As a horror buff, I knew that there were words you just don't say. "I'll be right back" and "Let's go check that noise out" are the biggest ones to avoid.

"Jesus H. Tits. If I go out there, will you just shut up about it and get back to work?"

I nodded. Martinez went back to reading his book, and X went back into her office. Matthews grabbed his rifle and locked his computer. He motioned for me to lead the way out the door, and I obliged. Hesitantly, I opened the giant steel door, slipping out into the darkness. SGT Matthews followed behind. His body language gave off the feeling that he thought I was an idiot, but he followed me anyway.

We made our way down the dirt path, passing by the motor pool that contained most of the Engineer unit vehicles.

"Here?" He asked.

I pointed forward. We continued down the road and rounded the corner. After a few more moments of walking, I stopped. I felt like something was wrong. I looked around and knew where I was. I was standing almost exactly where this thing was standing.

"He was right here. Or it. Whatever it was. They went up and over the wall over there," I said as I pointed to the spot where I saw this thing crawl over the wall.

"Ok, well, the guard tower just over there would have seen anyone coming away, or towards the wall, I'm sure it's fine. You're just seeing things from the lack of sleep," SGT Matthews said.

It made sense. I was a little sleep-deprived, as was everyone else tonight. We made our way back to headquarters. Neither of us spoke to each other the whole way. I said nothing out of embarrassment that perhaps I really was losing it from lack of sleep. He said nothing probably out of anger and lack of rest. We returned, and SGT Matthews immediately dismissed the concerns of Martinez and X.

"Nothing. There ain't nothing out there. Y'all go back to work please," Matthews unenthusiastically ordered.

It was a little disappointing to know that I was the only one to see this thing, but at the same time, it was a relief. I was losing my mind from lack of sleep. We already get so little out here, so it easily could be the culprit. I made my way back to my desk and unlocked my computer. It was finished booting up, and I was able to watch something to take my mind off of everything. The perk of being a runner is that I really don't have a purpose until there is a purpose. I run to other headquarters and hand-deliver things, pick up items, that sort of thing.

I scrolled through everything I had, but nothing really stuck out. I wanted something that I could lose myself in. I found some superhero television show and began to marathon watch the first season. I was starting to nod off around the second episode. I grabbed some water and tried to stay awake through my shows. Martinez thumbed through more of his novel. I could tell he was at a good part, as he would put his face closer to the book any time there was some action happening.

Maybe it made the scene better to read it closer? I never knew.

# Chapter 3

*FOB Centurion, IZ*
*0700 Local*
*February 11, 2010*

I woke up at my desk. I jerked awake violently, after realizing I had fallen asleep. The show was still playing, but I had no idea what was going on. I wiggled the cursor over the video. Episode five. Holy shit, I was asleep that long? I stopped the video and checked the time. Seven in the morning. Well, the good news is, this shift is over. The bad news is that I lost several hours of my life against my will. SGT Matthews was across the room, still using the computer. He was no longer watching cartoons. He was surfing the latest updates and messages from the base alerts.

Martinez was no longer at his post on the radio either. I assumed he went to get a morning smoke or take a leak at the latrine across the road. It was hard to know if X was in her office or not because she'd always close the door. I stood up from my desk, cracking my back and just about every other joint I owned. The chair was nice, but it was hell to sleep in. Matthews didn't say a word about me being wholly racked out in my seat. I guess he assumed we were all bound to catch some extra sleep at some point. I just took a few extra hours than anticipated.

I wandered over to the supply office. I gave it a quick knock before

I grabbed the door. No answer. I let myself in and peered around. X wasn't in the office. The sign that was left stuck to the back of the monitor was clear as day. "Gone to Gym. Back Ltr." Who knew how late that later would be, but she's at the gym. That's cool. Probably a good idea for me to get ready to do the same in a few once my relief shift arrives.

The replacement crew came in about a half-hour past seven. They were late, but given the situation of the other day, and the rockets, I think it might be a day or so before we all level out. We debriefed the crew on the nothingness that occurred. I dared not tell them about the roach man that skittered last night. I didn't see anything, and I'm positive my brain was making things up. Honestly, had someone been there, they would have said something to me. Alternatively, if it were a bug monster from Mars, it would have eaten my skull or something. It made sense to me, at least.

X strolled back into the building as we were packing our personal belongings. She was clearly at the gym for quite some time last night. X looked visibly exhausted but satisfied. She had sweat glistening from just about every pore that existed on her body, and the sweat rings on her clothing to match. Had Alexopolous not sported a short crop haircut, I'm sure her hair would have been matted down with sweat. As she came in, she opened the door to her office, slapping the top of the doorframe with both hands as she entered. A sure sign of someone coming down from a good workout, I'd imagine.

SGT Matthews and I finished chatting and joking around with the day shift replacements and made our way to our vehicle. Dancer was always parked just out back of the building, only a few paces off from the large steel doors that covered the rear entrance to the headquarters. There was a large cargo canopy netting draped over the rear of the building. It provided some refuge from the scorching hot Iraq sun for those day walkers. We appreciated it because on rare occasions our command staff would force us to sit through someone's award ceremony or other commendation reason. Or just to chew our asses off as a unit. Being under the mesh shade really changed the temperature drastically, believe it or not. It made those ass chewing's slightly bearable.

X joined us out back, followed by SPC Martinez. He had just finished a morning run after his shift change. I envied that guy, with his ability to just pick up weights and run a mile or two holding them. I was lucky if I could lift myself. It wasn't that I was out of shape or overweight. I just didn't have the arms for combat. Don't get me wrong. I was in better shape now than I had been before enlistment, but in comparison to my peers; I was a weak duck. What I lacked in physicality, I made up for in work ethic.

The four of us piled into the tan hunk of junk we called a vehicle. Matthews turned the starter crank, and the engine fired up with a loud, thunderous roar. These vehicles didn't allow you to just sneak away and get into shenanigans. Everyone for three blocks was aware you were moving it. It was so thunderously loud, our commander, Captain Seeker, came to see us off. He had missed us on the shift change and was a big talker. It's not that we didn't like the guy, we loved him to death. He lived an exciting life as a former professional wrestler. I don't mean the high school grapple and tackle wrestling. I'm talking flying elbows and atomic leg drop wrestling. He stood about six foot seven and must have been well into the mid to upper two hundred in weight. He was a big guy, and I wouldn't want to be on the receiving end of a clothesline from him.

He stalked up to the vehicle and thrust his head inside the unzipped plastic windows of my door.

"You fellas headed to get some chow?" He said excitedly.

"Roger that, sir. We can squeeze you in if you'd like to ride out and save you a walk," SGT Matthews said, leaning over me as to allow CPT Seeker to hear him over the roar of the engine.

His face lit up like a kid at Christmas. It wasn't like he couldn't go out and grab his own food or get there himself. He seemed genuinely excited to be tagging along with us. Martinez opted to give up his seat and hid in the back of the canvass covered trunk space. It was more of a short truck bed than anything, really. CPT Seeker ran into the building and returned a few moments later with his gear. We couldn't drive around without our helmets and vests on, base policy. He squeezed his massive body into the rear passenger seat behind SGT Matthews. The engine roared as Matthews placed his foot on the throttle and crept across the rock covered drive area toward the road.

The weather was a little milder today. Usually, I had a reason to bitch and complain about the temperature being too hot in February, but today, it felt more like a beautiful spring day. There was a breeze, and the sun didn't cook my face as much as it usually did through the windows. Looking out of my windows as we drove, I saw soldiers going about their daily taskings. The mechanics were working in their mechanic's bays, presumably pretending to fix the same vehicle until their shift was over. We passed by a troop of soldiers out for a unit run. They didn't really like us to do that because that resulted in too many of us in close proximity; easy pickings for a bad guy with the right kind of gun.

We didn't really talk much while we drove. This was mostly due in part from the loud roaring engine that we sat behind. I'm sure a part of that had to do with exhaustion, as I saw X was asleep in her chair when I looked back into the cab. Captain Seeker was all smiles but maintained his officer composure at the same time. This was his first deployment, and he was still enjoying the sights and sounds of what accompanied the trip. I could only assume Martinez was passed out in the back as well. He liked to grab a nap where he could, at least, when he wasn't reading his latest ranch bang fest novel.

As we passed by the airfield, we saw a large group of soldiers departing. They didn't look like they were armed to the teeth for a strike, so they may have just been flying out to a different base. It's tough to make out what type of people are there since we all wear the same damn thing. The DFAC crept into view over the hill as Dancer strained to make it up the incline. SGT Matthews and I gave it a gentle pat on the inside chassis, in the hopes that loving encouragement would keep it from stalling mid-climb. The vehicle crept over the hill, and we eventually settled it at our usual parking spot, near the giant concrete Jersey barrier. As if by routine, our passengers woke up and began to climb out of the Humvee. I was just thankful the shift was over, and I could eat. There wasn't much to do out in this country other than work out and eat. What a life.

Once I was outside of the vehicle, I felt an odd feeling. For whatever reason, I had a flash of what I saw last night on my walk. I rested my hands on my rifle, which was strapped to me as I recalled exactly what I saw. I'm not sure why it flashed in front of me, but things do that sometimes.

"Chantry! Get your head out of your ass and come on!" I heard called from behind.

I turned around and realized just about everyone had gone inside, and I was the only jackhole sitting in the sand daydreaming. I double-timed it as a hoofed over to join the group. I was ready to eat, and breakfast was calling my name.

We followed our usual routine, grabbing trays and dispersing to our respective meal choice locations. I made my obvious choice of the breakfast bar. This time, rather than getting the omelet as I've grabbed in the past, I loaded up on as many scrambled eggs, bacon and hash browns I could get. I was starving, and I didn't know why. I swung through the condiment area, grabbing handfuls of hot sauce as I passed through. I pocketed a cola from the fridge and made my way to our table.

"That was a long shift," Matthews said as he sat down, "I'm ready to pass the hell out."

I nodded in agreeance. I kept trying to push the Skitter Critter I saw last night out of my brain. Maybe that's what we can call it, you know? A Skitter Critter. I mentally coined the phrase to myself in case I ever saw it again or had a dream about it. At least I could give it a name for reference. Martinez slapped his tray down next to me and seated himself.

"Man, they didn't have no damn hummus today. This place is like a prison, yo," Martinez said as he shoved a fork into his salad.

"It's not a prison, specialist, it's worse. It's the Army," SGT Matthews said.

"Yeah, but they could at least take care of my ass while I'm out here. I'm risking my life and all, it's the least they could throw my way, feel me?"

I smiled at Martinez's complaints. A small part of me agreed with him. However, I at least had the predisposition mentality that we weren't supposed to live like kings either. X barely said any words, and CPT Seeker was still loading food onto his plate. I figured he was a big man, therefore, a big appetite. After overloading his plate, he grabbed a chocolate milk and joined our clan.

"Fellas." He said as he sat down. Before he could correct himself, X gave him an approving nod, as he realized she was sitting with us.

"I have to find something for us to do. How about some fitness-based training today?" SGT Matthews said.

I looked up from my eggs. I hated physical anything. If it involved anything other than watching movies and playing video games, I could almost guarantee you that my hand won't be first to volunteer for it.

"What you got lined up big sarge?" Martinez said, spewing shreds of lettuce from his mouth with each hard consonant he spoke.

"Parkour," Matthews said with a smile.

"I don't know if you are authorized to do that, Sergeant Matthews," Captain Seeker added.

"Sir, it's not going to be too crazy. We might go as far as climbing over some barricades in the base. Most of the stuff we hit will be waist-high. I've already mapped out a route."

Captain Seeker grunted in approval. He didn't seem enthusiastic, but he didn't forbid it either.

After we finished our food, we returned to the vehicle. Martinez stepped off to the side for his usual after-meal smoke. CPT Seeker found himself already strapped into the seat, gear on and ready to go.

I was prepared to just run for a bit and pass out in my bed. The only downside with being night shift is that all of the training exercises and other fun things take place exclusively for the day shift. We would either wake up earlier or go to bed later just to use a lot of the facilities. Martinez wrapped up his smoke, and everyone piled into Dancer. The engine started with no issue today, which was surprising. Typically, we would find ourselves cursing and pouring water on the engine until it cooperated with us. The lot of us headed back to headquarters to drop off the captain. We waved him off, said our farewells, heading back to The Village. We still needed to change out of our gear into something that we could run around in.

We changed rather quickly. Everyone was doing their own individual stretching outside of the entrance of The Village. Matthews joined us, ready to run. The overall consensus was clear: No one wanted to do this today.

"Come on! Just follow the path I take, try to step on what I do. It's not going to be too crazy. Yell if there's an issue. Oh, and don't break yourselves. I don't want to explain to the medics how you were injured," ordered Matthews.

The path was grueling. We started off simple; running across logs, short wide barriers, and large spans of flat land. Once we rounded the first corner, we jogged in place to ensure everyone could catch up.

"Ready to kick this up? I've been playing a ton of Assassin's Creed, and we are about to do the thing," Matthews said as he took off in the direction of a sizeable six-foot barrier.

SGT Matthews scaled the barrier with ease. He put one foot into the left side of it and pulled himself up to the top of it. I watched him do this as if he was practicing this move before ever dreaming of dragging our sorry carcasses out to witness. X was next. She hesitantly jogged over to the barrier, jumping up to reach the top. She pulled herself onto the top of the platform with ease. Martinez spit on the ground before taking off at a dead sprint. He rushed to the barrier and followed the path Matthews did, throwing one foot up for leverage. He rolled onto the top. Now it was my turn.

I started jogging to the barrier, sizing it up as much as possible. I was about six-foot-tall, so the barrier was at least eye level to me. I figure, with a decent jump, a foot into the side for grip, I'll jump right up. I approached the barrier, pushing off with my toes into a leap. My right foot dug into the side of the wall, but something was wrong. Something was very wrong. I tried to get a grip on the top of the barrier, but I had nothing to boost me up. I lost my foothold because I used the wrong foot. Idiot. How could I be so dumb? What didn't help my case is that now the rest of my squad was looking down on me trying to hang on for dear life, lest I fall three feet to the dirt.

I struggled and strained to pull myself up onto the barrier. I didn't have it in me to hoist my body up and over. I tried my best to slowly lower myself to not crash entirely to the ground. I almost didn't want to look up at the disappointed faces above me.

"Christ Chantry, you had one job," SGT Matthews grunted out.

I knew that he wasn't happy about me bypassing the obstacle, but it was the only way we were going to move forward. I tried a few additional attempts to mount this barrier, but it was for nothing. It was best that we all just keep going forward and finish today's session.

After running on a few more waist level obstacles and completing several sprinting exercises, we rounded out our adventure in front of The Village. Matthews didn't say much to me. He may have been too mad to say anything, or hopefully moved on and forgot about the whole thing. I highly doubt it was the latter.

"That was actually a blast!" X said as she tried to catch her breath.

Martinez gave a thumbs up of approval. He didn't really say anything verbally, but it seems he enjoyed himself too.

I was the only one that didn't struggle for breath. I was a runner by design, as I mentioned. This event today showed I was not built for strength. This was clearly displayed repeatedly after the several times my squad mates had to hoist me up and over other barriers along the way. Matthews finally was able to cool his breathing to be able to speak.

"Ok. Good stuff out there. X, next time we hit this course, I want to see faster running. Push yourself! Martinez, good shit. Chantry,

well, we may have to work on pushups, pull-ups, and other upper body exercises in the future. Good effort and kudos for not giving up. Even if you have spaghetti noodles for arms."

After Matthews finished his pep talk after our exercise, we were dismissed. I was thankful because I was just exhausted. I took what felt like the best shower of my life and went to my room for a much-needed sleep. I had no issue drifting off to sleep this morning, and that was a relief because I needed all of the rest I could get.

# Chapter 4

*FOB Centurion, IZ*
*2100 Local*
*February 11, 2010*

I awoke from my bed as I always did; covered in sweat. The stupid air conditioner didn't cooperate through the day and apparently had given out. I peeled myself out of the blankets and slugged my way over to the shower facilities. I removed the sweat I had accumulated from my body and moved to put my gear on. I prepared my brain for another twelve-hour shift ahead. I shuffled my body over to the pickup spot, waiting for SGT Matthews. Martinez was trudging through the desert sands in my direction. He didn't say any words, but I could tell his body was sore. He gently eased himself against a barricade, lighting up his cigarette before he rested against the structure. X was nowhere to be found.

I decided to look around a bit in the area for her. My body ached just as much as Martinez. I already started off in a bad mood from waking up overheated. As I rounded the corner, I slammed headfirst into X.

"Jesus, fuck! What the hell, man?" She yelled as she jumped back.

"My bad. Sorry about that. I just wanted to know where you were. SGT Matthews should be here in a sec," I responded back to her, embarrassed that we almost collided.

It wasn't until she walked around me to join Martinez that I noticed she was limping a bit. She seemed a little stiff and sore like the rest of us. Already I could tell today was going to be one hell of a day. Probably the worst day of our lives. Little did I know what was waiting for us around the corner, just moments later.

Matthews rolled up in Dancer. He seemed more chipper than usual, and that frankly rubbed the rest of us the wrong way. We all looked and felt like death. Thinking about it, he has been running that trail, preparing to run us at some point. It makes sense that his muscles were already trained for the course at this point. We climbed into the Humvee as best as we could. The three of us tried to stifle our groans and grunts as we slid into the vehicle. My rifle banged into my thigh, and I thought that was the end of me. I didn't realize I used these body parts that much for climbing.

We followed our typical routine, once more. This was almost like a computer program that is designed to repeat a scenario over and over until it reaches the end of the code. This was our lives; wake up, eat, work, eat, and sleep. I dragged myself to the tray pickup in the DFAC. I made my way to my usual breakfast bar when, to my horror, there was no breakfast. I told you that this day was the worst day of my life. I settled on some grilled chicken and rice and found our seats.

"So, gang, how you all feeling today?" SGT Matthews asked, his face beaming with excitement that we ran his stupid obstacle course.

X grunted. I don't blame her. Every muscle ached. Even my voice was sore. Martinez joined us a few moments later and slowly eased himself down into the bench seat.

"I'll take that as it went well. We can rerun the course next week. I have some new ideas I'd love to implement," Matthews said as he shoveled a mouthful of noodles into his face.

The three of us shot a glance at each other. We were on the same page with how we felt and were anything but enthusiastic about doing it again at this point. The rest of our feast was spent shifting in our seats, trying not to strike up any soreness. Afterward, the squad moved back to Dancer and loaded in. Martinez appeared too sore to stand around for a smoke and opted to just ease into the seat of the Humvee.

Shift change at headquarters proved unfruitful again. Nothing crazy. No attacks or rockets were logged. We were changing over to our night shift roles, setting up our laptops, and logging into the work computers. Martinez took his post by the radio, continuing his romance book from yesterday. Yet another routine day, in this mundane job. Join the Army, they said. See the world they said. Yeah, I see a desk and sand. Lifechanging.

About an hour into the shift, Studds burst into the room. He looked like he might have run over. The guy wasn't out of shape, but he may have been on foot for some time. Studds was red in the face, sweat pooling on his forehead.

"Man, that door is like, super heavy!" He let out a bit of a laugh as he said it, looking back at the steel door.

I always thought Studds reminded me of that character Jim Brewer played on Half Baked. Or maybe Spicoli from Fast Times. For a guy who wasn't high, he sure as hell talked like it. He had that 'stoner speak.' Studds was about my height, just a little over six foot. He was slightly above average build, blonde hair. He wasn't oversized, but damn if he wasn't hitting the gym trying to be. I looked up from my desk to see him coming down the ramp into the building. Martinez saw him too.

"Sup Holmes!" He called out to Studds, giving him a nod of acknowledgment.

Studds walked straight over to SGT Matthews. He had a note in his hand, which he passed over to Matthews. SGT Matthews flipped it open and read through it. He picked up the phone.

"What the hell do you mean you guys have been trying to call for the past hour? The phone hasn't rung once," Matthews said as he held the receiver to his head while jiggling the hook a few times.

His expression changed a bit after fiddling with it for a few moments. I got up and decided to knock on X's door. She answered, earbuds in.

I made the hand motion for a phone and pointed over to her desk. She shook her head but pulled her headphones out.

"What? No. I haven't called you guys," X responded, slowly working to replace the earbud.

"No, not that. Does your phone work?" I asked, trying to push past to access it.

X didn't really like other people in the office. There were a lot of materials that had to be accounted for, and it was a liability to have me in there. It didn't stop me. I grabbed the phone and placed it to my ear. Nothing. Completely silent.

"Fuck me, the internet is down too. Well, that means one of two things: either the systems took a shit on us, or someone killed themselves or died or something," Matthews cried from across the hall.

I wandered back over, X followed close. She was curious as to what was going on. Martinez was still in his position by the radio, feet kicked up on the desk. He was still nose deep into his smutty fantasy novel, I assumed.

"Probably the crappy wiring, sarge," Martinez yelled out, not taking his eyes off his book.

X and I piled into the office that SGT Matthews and I shared. Studds was sitting in my chair.

"Well, move right in why don't ya?" I joked toward Studds.

"Don't mind if I do!" Studs breathed out, as he placed his feet on my desk, folding his hands behind his head.

We hadn't been in the office for more than a few moments together when we heard some frantic sounds coming from the outer hallway. It was radio chatter. We didn't have any missions logged to leave the base for a few more hours, so this was unusual.

"Sarge, you may want to come out here and handle this!" SPC

Martinez called out.

You could audibly hear his chair rock forward, the feet hitting the floor below him. It must have been serious. Everyone moved toward his direction and crowded around the radio. What we heard was barely audible, but I'm sure of what I heard.

*"...Foxtrot, Mike, Zulu niner.........Everyone.......Not sure what........lock......ckdown the whole ba......the city. Repeat. The city is over......."*

The chatter went dead. Martinez grabbed the handpiece and engaged the button to speak.

"Repeat. Last transmission unclear. I did not copy. What is going on with the city? Lockdown? Repeat. Over." Martinez spoke.

I swear, whenever he grabbed the radio, he dumped his accent, any slang or verbal mannerisms. He spoke as if he worked talk radio in the fifties. I was too concerned by the message to be entranced by his vocal talents.

"...Mike, Zulu...er.....Dead. Ev.....suprise....lockdown the base....overrun....ity." The voice on the other end managed to get out enough before the entire transmission went dead.

"Jesus Christ. What do they mean to lockdown? I haven't heard any alarms," X said, stepping back toward her office door.

Martinez continued to fiddle with the radio to establish communication with anyone. He changed channels to try to get anyone who would hear him. After the third or fourth channel change, he got something. "Guns. Guns. Get the guns. They're coming over the walls. Repeat. Coming over the walls. Fucking Armageddon doomsday level shit." The new voice said.

It was the channel for the Cav Scout unit down the road. I kept replaying the transmission over and over in my head. *Get the guns.* It makes sense. I began to make my way over to my rifle, sitting behind my desk.

"Ok, I'm going to like, make my way back to my spot, and I'll hit you guys up over the radio after I get there," Studds said, as he started toward the large steel door.

"I don't recommend that. If there is some sort of lockdown that we missed, you don't want to be outside," requested SGT Matthews, also heading back toward his desk.

"I don't know about y'all, but I'm fixin' to head back to the gym for a bit after this whole thing blows over. I took some pre-workout mix before coming here. I was going there afterward. I'm getting the shakes, man. I gotta lift something."

Studds slung his M4 rifle over his shoulder. He gave us his best bow before grabbing the door. The large door always squealed with every open. It was mostly due to it sticking to the concrete floor, almost resting on it. Obviously, weight was a factor, but so was rust. Things were so mistreated out here, I'm surprised the building hasn't come down on us yet.

I watched as Studds headed out the door, waving to him as he backed out into the street behind him. Then, out of the shadows, I saw it. It looked like the thing I saw before, but a little different this time. Before I could call out to Studds to let him know the Skitter Critter was behind him, it had leaped into the air. I could vaguely make out claws. At least, I think they were claws. It didn't matter what they were because they were about to take hold of one of my combat buddies. I reached out my hand to point beyond Studds into the shadows. My throat was dry and unable to conjure up speech. I tried to yell out.

By the time words could escape my mouth, Studds had been snatched away from the door. In what seemed like hours, I watched one of the guys I knew get whisked away as if he was a featherweight. Once this thing moved back into the shadows, I uttered a noise.

"Shit! Shit! Shit! It got Studds!" I screamed, backing into the office to join SGT Matthews.

"Who got what? Calm down," Matthews said, doing his best to get an answer out of me.

I was in a terrible condition. I could barely get a grasp on what happened myself, let alone the ability to explain it. The scene replayed in my mind over and over like the movie of a bad nightmare. The vision of Studds getting pulled away from the door as if he weighed nothing frightened me. It meant these things were strong and could whisk any one of us away at a moment's notice. Luckily I didn't have to spew words out of my face, as Martinez blasted past me. He slammed his hands down on SGT Matthews' desk.

"They took Studds, B!", Martinez shrieked through a cracking voice,

"They grabbed him! Some space alien motherfucker!"

He seemed as frantic as I did. The only difference is that he was able to articulate his words where I was a frozen chicken. I watched as SGT Matthews stood up from his chair, adjusting his gaze in my direction.

"Is this what you're trying to say? What's going on?" He asked.

"I don't know! It was one of those things I told you about from my walk. I swear," I frantically tried to calm myself and articulate a competent thought through my lips.

SGT Matthews grabbed his rifle, slinging it over his shoulder as he moved toward the giant steel door. He sauntered over, seemingly careless that a giant monster could eat his face at any moment. Actually, I'm not sure what these things could even do. I'm sure it wasn't good either way. We grabbed our assigned weapons and followed Matthews toward the door. I stood just inches behind Martinez and was sandwiched in by a curious X, who missed the action.

"Jesus, can I get some room to breathe?" Matthews said as he placed his hand on the door.

He was right. If something tried to get him, we were literally forming a blockade. That's horror movie 101, don't block your exits. Honestly, we were already breaking like a hundred rules in the book by even investigating this situation. But that's Hollywood. This is real life.

As we backed down the ramp a few steps, Matthews put some weight on the door. It groaned and squealed with its disgusting metallic sound once again. Anything within a hundred feet knew we were coming out of that door, thanks to the cacophony of sounds coming from it. SGT Matthews peered out into the darkness of the night. He looked left, right, up, and down. His expression changed as he poked back into the building, letting the door close behind him.

"Ok, so, what am I missing? Are you guys messing with me right now?" Matthews said, annoyed that we may have been playing a prank. We did love our shenanigans.

Before any of us could assure him that this was not a game, his expression changed once more. It was no longer a face of anger and frustration. What replaced his appearance was now a look of disgust and concern. He looked down at his hands. We could see his hands as well. Blood. There was sticky, dripping blood on his right hand. The very one that pushed open the door to look outside. He brushed his hand over the doorway once more. It was coated in blood near the seam of where the door met the frame. My heart sank into my tan combat boots. This cannot be real.

Martinez immediately hit the radios. He scanned all of the broadcast channels and listened in. There was barely anything audible as everyone talked over each other. What was apparent, however, was the sense of dread every one of us felt listening to that audio. Every soldier dispatching the same transmission. They all cried out of some monster, or a creature of sorts. No one dared called them Skitter Critters, however. That was all mine.

The transmissions began to die out little by little. One by one, the soldiers stopped talking as if they were being snuffed out systematically.

"What the hell," Matthews said, as he breathed in a deep breath.

I shut down. I was utterly useless to everyone. I found myself inside my own brain trying to comprehend what was going on. We were only a few months shy of coming home from this godforsaken

country, why the hell does something like this have to go down?

"Chantry!"

I heard my name called out, snapping me back to this world once more. I must have been visibly zoned out.

"Yo!" I responded as if trying to play off my fear.

"We have to get the hell out of here. I don't know where we have to go, but we have to go," Matthews said.

He was checking his weapon. I assume to ensure it wasn't jammed.

He also pulled out the magazine from his IBA vest. We weren't allowed to keep ammo locked and loaded, but we could have it on our person. He checked the two magazines from his body armor, pushing the rounds down to ensure they weren't jammed. It's almost like he's done this before.

None of the four of us had seen combat. We were desk jockeys. We weren't built for this sort of thing. It seemed SGT Matthews had the right idea, as we all began to run inventory on our ammo, weapons, and supplies.

"We don't have enough to hole up in this building, that's apparent," SGT Matthews said, "So we gotta get moving. If any of you guys have suggestions, I'm all ears."

I couldn't get a reasonable thought across my brain. Everything I thought went straight to every action movie I watched. None of those scenarios seemed logical, physically possible, or worth uttering from my face.

"We should get bigger guns. Can we make it to the armory?" Martinez said.

I was impressed with his thinking. I agree, bigger guns might be a good idea. I was also a believer in more ammo. The downside is that more ammo equals more weight, and we were already weighed down with all of this equipment as it was.

"Hey, X, you got the key to the armory across the way?", Matthews called out across the hall.

X was busy digging through her office for anything that could be remotely useful. The shuffling came to a halt as she poked her arm out of the room, holding what looked like a key to that armory. SGT Matthews nodded. He grabbed some paper from the laser printer across from him, resting on a line of file cabinets. With his left hand, he motioned for us to join him.

Martinez and I huddled around this paper. We watched as Matthews drew a crude version of our headquarters cul-de-sac. We were tucked away, with the main road cutting through us. To our left, an abandoned warehouse. To our right, the portable crappers. Directly across the street, however, lay the goldmine we desired. The Armory. Based on memory, there wasn't a single barrier or obstacle to move and cover from.

"Ok, so this is what we got. Nothing. There is literally nothing in the way. This is a good thing and a bad thing. We are going to have to sprint over as quickly as possible. The good news is that nothing will be in our way to get there. The bad news, however, is that it's a nonstop run for almost two hundred feet," SGT Matthews said, pointing to the marks on his drawing.

He sketched out a rough plan for us to follow on this paper from his desk drawer. It seemed logical from where I stood, at least. After all, he was the boss man. X came over with a cardboard box full of necessities. She had several chem-lights, flashlights, and zip-ties. I was about to question the zip ties, but I realized they probably would serve a purpose at some point.

She didn't have any type of food to pack.

It actually dawned on me, given the lack of food to pack, that we were almost due for our usual mealtime. I lost so much track of time. Due to the excitement, I also lost track of my stomach. Giving thought to eating actually made me hungry. I hadn't been hungry or at least thought I was hungry before now. I made my way to the cookies we had stashed at headquarters. They would have to do for now.

I returned back to the war room with a face full of cookies. I must have missed something critical because everyone was geared up. They donned their helmets, IBA vests, and were strapped into their weapons.

"Well, shit. Give me a second," I called to the team, spewing chunks of a minty flavored chocolate cookie everywhere.

I strapped on my vest and helmet. I always hated wearing this heavy gear. I assumed the helmet was going to give me neck problems one day. I double-checked the vest, making sure I had my pouches and other things I required storage. I probably had about six magazine pouches on my vest, in addition to some pouch for first aid gear. It was void of any first-aid materials but could easily be used for storage.

I decided to stash a few handfuls of the cookies into that pouch. You never know when you'll need some sort of food, right?

The room felt tense. We had never felt this level of intensity since we deployed, even with the rockets coming in. Now that I'm thinking about it, we haven't had our daily shower of booms all night. Typically, we would have been scheduled a partly cloudy with a chance of missiles twice by now. But it was silent out there. The thought flitted across my mind, but it was extinguished by the commands of SGT Matthews.

"You ready to do this? Martinez, you're the fastest runner. You take point. X, you follow after three seconds. Chantry, you'll follow X. The same three seconds apply. I'll bring up the rear. Good?" SGT Matthews said.

We each nodded. The four of us put a clenched fist out, giving a giant fist bump before turning to face the giant steel door. The door groaned slightly as the winds of the Middle East blew past them. I thought to myself *that's not ominous at all.* Slowly, Martinez crept toward the door. He extended a fingerless gloved hand out to rest his palm on the cold metal. Martinez looked back toward the group, as if for affirmation that everyone was ready. His gaze returned to the door as he pressed into the door. As usual, the door groaned with a loud squeal as it popped out from its resting position. It swung open wide. Martinez took a few steps forward, scanning the street on either side for activity.

My heart nearly pounded out of my chest. The butthole pucker factor was high. That was how we typically rated the intensity of activities. The higher the pucker factor, the more dangerous it was. On a scale of one to ten, this pucker factor was a solid twenty-two. Martinez tactically shuffled toward the building across the road. The road seemed wider today than any other day. I watched as X silently counted and followed suit. She scanned left to right as she tactically hustled across the street. Christ, it was my turn. I was not ready.

I began to count in my head to three. *One. Two. Fuck. Me.* I moved forward out of the safety of the building. I noticed a puddle near the door, on its right side. I tried not to think about what that was filled with. I moved forward at a steady shuffle. I wanted to look around at my surroundings but figured it best to not see what is out there. I focused on the back of X's vest. I noticed Martinez had made it to the door and took a defensive stance. He faced the left side of the building, looking out into the road. X made it shortly after and copied the same position on the right. I stumbled my way to the door of the building. I turned slightly to look back at SGT Matthews.

He was making his way to our position, but much slower than we were. I was actually surprised by how quick we moved, considering how sore our bodies were from that parkour session. It's amazing what adrenaline and fear will do to the human body for survival. I already knew I'd be feeling this later. He looked up at our position. He slowed his movements to almost a slow walk. I watched as his hand raised and pointed to the left part of the rooftop of the neighboring warehouse building. I struggled to look through the dusty haze the wind created with the sand. And then I saw it. On the roof, something was watching us. It was crouching down, almost in a gargoyle stance from a fancy New York rooftop back home.

Matthews reached into his vest pouch. I noticed he withdrew a small shiny object. It was the armory key, dangling from the lanyard it was housed on within the supply office. I think we all knew without saying a word what he was about to do. I glanced back up at the creature, now in more of a pounce position. I was able to see more of it now in the faint moonlight. It appeared to have a small tail. Its body housed at least two legs and two arms by my count. I could see the rubble crumbling off of the rooftop where it's giant talon-like claws dug in for grip. Each of us had fifteen bullets. Matthews knew the odds. We didn't even know what we were dealing with.

As we watched the armory key and his fifteen round magazine soar through the air in our direction, the creature leaped from its perch. Claws outstretched, it let out a shrill roar-like scream. It was nothing I'd ever heard before. It was as if a lion and an elephant had a baby, and that baby got punched in the junk pre-roar. The keys landed inches in front of Martinez, the magazine landing just in front of me. As Martinez fumbled with the key, we looked back in horror as our leader, our friend, was ripped to shreds before our eyes. We assumed the same fate for Studds, even though it was never witnessed.

# Chapter 5

*FOB Centurion, IZ*
*0230 Local*
*February 12, 2010*

The armory door jerked open as SPC Martinez threw his full weight into it. Neither X or myself dared squeeze off a round into this thing. We knew it could draw more. What were the odds this was a lone wolf? The two of us slipped through the giant door, closing it behind us. There were no windows, and barely any light in this room. Luckily for us, X prepared a survival kit. We were all handed flashlights before crossing the road. I fumbled around in my vest pouches for the light. We each pressed the torches on, their beams illuminating the room in a bright LED glow. Jackpot.

There were shelves upon shelves of items. Cases of ammo littered the floor, as we hardly felt like putting anything away after a rifle range visit. Spare weapons hung in the racks, waiting for the day we had to qualify marksmanship once again with it. X made her way to the M249B, a massive, belt-fed machine gun. Not my cup of tea, this thing was too unwieldy for me. I preferred lightweight weaponry. I noticed the rack of M9 handguns off to my right. That was more my pace. Give me mag-fed versus belt-fed any day.

Martinez eyed up the handguns with me. He drew two of them for himself. The thought never dawned on me to take more than one thing. Honestly, my goal was to grab handfuls of ammunition and shoot my way out of here. I never considered the thought that an extra weapon or two may come in handy. None of us said a word in this room. I noticed we all did our best to focus on the loot before us. It was probably better that way because the first word one of us said would easily trigger waterworks in mourning for SGT Matthews.

I grabbed handfuls of empty magazines out of one of the cardboard boxes. I checked the spring in them, making sure they at least functioned. They checked out. I scanned the room for the first open ammo case. I don't know why I was trying to be respectful and only using one that was already opened. I guess we were trained to start from the open container, it's just a reflex at this point. I saw the brown box labeled "5.56," and made my way over. I dumped my armful of magazines onto the shelf just below and tore into the cardboard box.

I grabbed about ten or twelve clips of ammunition. I sat down on a large wooden crate and began to load up the empty magazines, placing them on the shelf next to the ammo box.

"Hey, I'm going to load some mags for us," I whispered to the team.

Martinez shot me a thumbs up. He was already loading up 9MM rounds into the M9 magazines. X was watching the door. She didn't say much. It was probably a good idea to have her watch the door anyhow, to cover our six.

We were as careful as we could as the two of us rattled our way through ammunition. It was a shame we didn't have anything larger in our unit. I'd kill for one of those shotguns like they use in all the video games. Was I ever going to watch another movie or video game? Hell, at this moment, I'm living in one of those right now.

X finagled around with her belt feeder. She made sure everything was ready to go at a moment's notice. The particular 249 she removed from the shelf had a nice little tripod to set the weapon down on for stability. Those were particularly nice to free up a hand if you needed it. I finished up stacking full magazines, loading myself up to capacity. I felt like I just used the ammo cheat codes. My vest could hold quite a bit of ammo, and I even loaded some up in the cargo pocket down by my ankle. You never know, right?

Martinez happened upon a box of unused holsters and pouches. We rummaged through and managed to salvage five pistol holsters and a few handgun magazine pouches. We affixed them to ourselves and loaded them up as well. I now sported two handguns and an M4 rifle. Honestly, I was a few steps away from being the main over-buffed character from some shoot-em-up game. But then I looked over at X, who now donned the M249 across her midsection. She let the M4 dangle off to her side and used one of the leg drop pistol holsters to carry the M9. I now felt inadequate.

Martinez used his two vest mounded pistol holsters to house the dual M9's he took. He still handled the M4 as his primary, however. We were armed to the teeth. I figured this was the part where we play the heroic music as we walk in slow motion through the exit to victory. We didn't have a plan. I waved over to get SPC Martinez' attention.

"Dude. What the hell are we doing?" I asked, still whispering.

"I don't know, B. Where should we take up? Who knows what's still left?" Martinez responded.

We sat there looking at each other for a few moments.

"The Base Exchange. We will go there," X muttered.

Honestly, it sounded like the best plan we had. We were all of equal rank here, so no one could pull rank on each other for an idea.

"We go there. The BX will have food and other supplies. We already have the guns, but we won't make it through the next day without everything else. I'm sure others already thought of it too. We'd be better in large numbers," X said as she stood up to signal it was time to leave.

"I say we make a move for the vehicle," Martinez said as he chambered a round into his rifle.

I nodded. At least we would make good time. The only fathomable downside is that the engine is so ungodly loud. We may

as well put a big sign over our heads that shows where we are. Apparently, X was on the same wavelength as me.
"What are you, fucking stupid?" She hissed to him.

Martinez shrugged and looked over at me. I shot him the look to indicate I thought it was a decent idea. We all knew grabbing Dancer would be a bad idea. That vehicle was absolute garbage even on a good day. Between the overheats, loud engine, and the mere fact it isn't an armored Humvee should be enough indicator that it's a wrong choice.

We didn't grab up all of these guns just to be killed.

Running the scenario of our deaths through my head managed to let the thought of SGT Matthews slip through. I felt my chest begin to flex in and out. Was I crying? Christ, I needed to get a hold of myself. I realized then that the wave of grief hit everyone. Hell, if we were going to ball like babies, may as well be in a private room in near darkness. Studds didn't deserve this either. He was a good dude and always looked out for everyone. He enjoyed being the clown of the unit when he could. I couldn't get the images of their deaths out of my heads. I kept seeing the creatures flash across my eyes as well.

*What the hell were these creatures?* I thought to myself over and over. I tried to assess their origin with my pop culture knowledge. They didn't appear to be zombies. At least, not at first glance. They didn't fit the bill. Aliens? They could easily have been alien. I've never seen anything like the Skitter Critter before, and I've marathoned a ton of Animal Planet specials. I wish I knew more about this. I'm going to label the Skitter Critter as an alien from a different planet until further notice. Jesus, this is literally pulled from the pages of some Hollywood script.

X eased her hand onto the handle of the door. It creaked slightly but nothing to the magnitude of our headquarters door. She pulled it slightly, allowing only an inch or two of an opening. I could tell she was doing her best to shift around to look at whatever of the outside world that she could see. Before I could even ask what she was seeing, she threw a hand up. Extending from her clenched fist, she formed a thumbs up. We still didn't have a plan. X shut the door gently, stifling out any light that flooded the room from the moon outside.

"So, what the hell are we doing here?" Martinez grunted.

"Let's make our way to the gym. It's the closest building and probably safe," X said.

"This is no time to get in a few pumps with the weights, X," I joked.

No one laughed. Actually, the gym isn't a bad pick. It wasn't too far down the road, and it takes us closer to the Base Exchange building. In total, we had about two and a half miles to hoof it. It didn't sound bad on paper but add the element of these monsters, and that may as well be a three-day journey. We three looked at each other.

"Gym?" X said.

"Gym," Martinez and I said in unison.

X pulled the door back open a little more this time. She peered out into the sandy, empty street ahead. It appeared clear. We did our best to recall our Army training. We stacked on the door as if we were about to conduct a strike. Our weapons were locked and loaded, and our hearts racing. One by one, we slipped out of the door into the cold air of the early morning.

The trio of us immediately began scanning our sectors. We looked high, low, and everywhere in between for these things. The Critters could obviously climb, so an aerial attack wasn't out of the cards. I preferred when the bad guys were designed like us. We shuffled in a tight group over to the warehouse across the way. I glanced over at the pool of blood where SGT Matthews stood on the road. It wrenched my stomach a little, but I swallowed and pushed forward. We slammed up against the side of the warehouse, getting as tight as possible to the

wall. The road looked clear for as far as we could tell in the moonlight.

I really wished for daylight.

We shuffled in a tactical formation to the next building. We moved as a group because we already saw what happens if we are separated.

Is this the most tactical maneuver we could muster up? We moved double-time to the last building in the row. Our gear clanked and rattled as we moved as silent as possible over the dirt and rock-filled road. Pebbles crunched under our combat boots as we stepped through the night. X was first in the pack. She slammed her body against the building, preparing to peer around the corner. The three of us each took turns looking at our next destination. I hated flying blind and wanted to know where we were headed.

X pointed to the swimming facility, now drained, just beyond the traffic circle. The gym lies just beyond that building on its left. I've walked to the gym a million times during my shifts and not once did it feel this far away. We each looked around the area for signs of the Skitter Critters. It was pretty quiet out. There were no signs of these monsters. I assume there was more than one because let's be honest; if we as an Army were getting our asses handed to us by one of these things, we should just pack it in now. But what if it's invincible? What if this monster alien dude couldn't be killed by regular rounds? Are we nuke bound?

I was so wrapped up in my stupid thoughts that I nearly missed the signal to move forward. We shuffled across the vast stretch of road that went through the traffic circle. It was wrong. It felt unprotected. I couldn't wait until we made it to the pool house. I didn't like being this exposed. I was right for feeling that way, too. As X neared the far side of the traffic circle, she stopped. Martinez and I halted our pace as well. We each saw it. A Skitter Critter, just twenty or so meters ahead. It was snooping around in some trash. This one looked just like the one that I saw the other night, humanoid-shaped. It had a fully developed head, pronounced body, and very long legs. The only thing that gave it away was its unusually long legs. It was crouched down a bit, but you could tell they were long.

We stared in silence as it moved through the piles of garbage. It crawled over the mess with ease, using its claw-like hands to cling to the building. We were too fascinated by this close encounter to realize that another one of these guys was creeping up on our side. All too quickly, it lunged at X, and she hit the dirt with a thud. The creature recovered and thrust one sharp claw in her direction. She dodged the strike. Luckily, it only got her shoulder strap for the M249. She rolled away, drawing the M9 pistol she stashed on her vest. I guess this was it. We were going hot.

She fired three rounds center mass into the creature. We hoped the heart and essential parts were kept there. It recoiled back with the screech of a thousand car tires. X crawled back our direction but stopped in her tracks. For whatever reason, I looked behind us. Part of me was glad I did, while the other half of me regrets what I saw. A swarm of Skitter Critters of all shapes and sizes were coming our way. The way they moved felt like something out of that Alien movie. That didn't go well for the Marines, so I immediately checked out mentally. Soldier mode kicked in. I don't know what took over, but I stepped forward, reaching for X's weapon.

As I mounted the m249 machine gun against my shoulder, I felt the weight of the entire weapon. I had never really had the opportunity to fire one of these bad boys before, but by god, there was a first for everything. I flipped the safety selector switch, removing the weapon from safe. I closed my eyes for a brief moment, knowing time was of the essence. I reopened them, steadied my breathing as I squeezed softly on the trigger. I fired small round bursts into the crowd of these things. I barely knew how to work one of these because my military career thus far has been magazine-fed weapons. I prayed to whoever was listening for the belt to remain free with no snag. I continued to three to five-round burst my way to the base exchange. The good news: these things were going down with regular ammo. The bad news: I don't know if I have enough ammo for all of them.

I began to spray rounds downrange like it was nobody's business. Martinez also laid down fire while X recovered from the attack. She managed to whirl around with her M4 rifle and start taking shots into the crowd. It felt like there were hundreds of these things coming our way, but in reality, it may have been thirty to forty. They were dropping to the ground as they were struck with rounds. I think subliminally we all knew that we needed to get off the streets. We just rang the dinner bell in the middle of an open road.

As we fired our weapons, we began backing up toward the pool building. I felt my body hit up against it after several steps. The 249 jammed almost on cue. I never took the time to figure this thing out. Part of me had regrets at that moment, but the other half of me just opted to switch weapons. I switched out to the M4 rifle. Between the three of us, we must have burned through two hundred or more rounds. It wasn't until we stepped back toward the gym that we noticed their numbers thinned to single digits. The remaining dozen or so scattered off to different directions. Thank god, I was starting to get worried I was going to be out of ammo soon.

X looked back at me. She had some dirt over her face, but otherwise unharmed. For a badass, she had very soft features to her face. That must have been her superpower to let you off guard. The second you'd think about hitting on her, she'd take you to the ground and break at least three bones in the process. She didn't let on that getting tackled by a Skitter Critter bothered her. She simply reached out for her machine gun. I happily handed it over. The barrel was glowing a faint orange from discharging so many rounds through it. She took note to hold that end away from her body.

Martinez patted me on the shoulder, smiling as he passed. I'm not sure if that was in congratulations for surviving or for using the stupid machine gun. We cautiously walked our way through the fenced area that led to the gym. The fence was a tall steel structure, something placed here by the locals long before we went to war. We silently decided that talking wasn't necessary out here. We'd already caused enough of a racket with our firefight. My adrenaline was still pumping, and I could practically feel my heartbeat through my vest.

We reached the end of the pool building. It seemed clear all the way over to the gym. The gym itself was a bunker with small slit windows at the top. Honestly, X had a good idea to go here. The building lacked points of entry. With only about two or three doors leading in, the windows were small enough to keep those things from crawling through them. We slowly moved toward the structure, weapons lowered and relaxed but still gripped. We figured that those things must have been spooked by losing so many numbers at once. I know I'd be.

X slid her helmet off and placed an ear to the crack between the doors. Martinez and I halted and tried to not make a sound. After a moment or two, she waved for us to come to the door. She pulled the door open, and I stepped inside. Why did I decide to become a super soldier? Why am I going to go first? This wasn't my typical behavior. It must have been the adrenaline.

I didn't see anything in the hallway as Martinez brushed past me on my right. We each scanned any storage nook or cranny for anything that wasn't human. It was an uneventful search aside from the mop that scared the piss out of my body. It hit the ground with a loud, clacking sound. Thank god I wasn't quick on the trigger or I'd have killed a mop dead. We made it past the administration check-in desk. There was a little blood on the counter, but otherwise untouched.

The hallway was clear. The next stop was the gym itself. X took the liberty of putting the chain on the door and locking it. There was another set of doors at the other end of the hall, but if we could limit the entrances that we knew about, we'd have less to guard. The gym was starting to appear lit as the sun was rising outside. I pushed the swinging door open and stepped into the gym. Well, that's a relief. It's not a nest of these things. I was worried about a hive scenario in the back of my mind walking into this place.

"Sheeit. At least they don't got like a queen or something chillin' in here, right B?" Martinez said, and he checked my shoulder with his.

Glad I'm not alone in this thinking. The room was oddly still. We regrouped on the other side of the swinging door, inside the gym.

"Ok, so let's sweep the area, make sure all of the doors are locked, and nothing is waiting in the shadows. Martinez, you take the left down by the basketball hoops. Chantry, you go right, down by the bleachers. I'll check the latrines and meet up with you two here in a few," X commanded.

It would appear X was taking charge. That's not a bad thing considering I sure as hell didn't want the responsibility even though I was technically next in line behind SGT Matthews. I nodded to X and began scanning around as I made my way across the gym.

After a few meters, I stopped and looked back. X had disappeared around the corner to the latrines. Martinez was looking in the small storage closets that housed a lot of the sporting equipment. I was alone. I stepped slowly toward the bleachers. They were wooden and pushed out for seating. This also meant they had space to hide behind them. Any number of these creatures could be waiting in there for us. I proceeded with caution.

As I reached the end of the bleachers nearest the shortest step, I heard a noise. It was a shuffle of sorts, but it stopped suddenly. I glanced down at my rifle, deciding it was too large to take under the stairs practically. The smart choice was the M9. I slung my rifle as I drew my pistol. I checked the rounds, full magazine. I mentally psyched myself up to face whatever was under the stairs in the shadows, but I'm not stupid. I grabbed for my rifle once more and used the buttstock of the rifle to beat on the stairs twice. I slammed the butt down with a loud thud which echoed through the gym and resonated loudly under the stairs of the bleachers. Something moved. I wasn't sure what it was, but I let the rifle go and placed two hands to grip the pistol. I made out a figure in the shadows. I stepped back and took aim at the target. My heart was in my throat.

# Chapter 6

*FOB Centurion, IZ*
*0530 Local*
*February 12, 2010*

I removed the pistol from safe to ready with my thumb. I wasn't sure what was about to get me, but I damn sure wasn't going to go easily. I stepped back once more, now standing in a beam of light that shone through the window slat.

"Chantry? That you, man?" A voice asked shakily.

"Yeah. Identify!" I commanded.

"Yeesh. Calm down there, Robocop. It's me," the voice said, as PFC Dalog crawled out from his hiding spot.

I looked him over. He wasn't even in his Army Combat Uniform. He was in the Physical Training outfit. It appears he was probably sleeping or enjoying his downtime in his PT's when the proverbial shit hit the fan.

"Wow. Let me just say that you rolling in here looking like goddamn Rambo armed to the teeth is hilarious. Secondly, can I get one of them there guns? I mean, you got two of em," Dalog asked.

I looked down at myself, realizing I really was armed to the teeth. I placed the handgun on safe and handed it over to Dalog. He was a little against the grain, like me. He didn't fully conform to the soldier mindset like most others we knew. He was my gaming buddy when we were back home. We'd frequently be found in the barracks playing video games rather than out partying and drinking with the rest of the group.

Dalog was a little stocky. He wore glasses that fit almost entirely around his face. He was Asian or something, but we never really cared to discuss anyone's origins. Once you're a soldier, you're a damn soldier. I think I remember in passing he said he was from the islands or something. He didn't have an accent though, he was American born and raised.

I had to come up with a way to let him know about Studds. I know the two of them were good buddies. I can recall several times where PFC Studds would call Dalog late at night just to drunkenly talk to him. He was one of the few that would actually take those calls and hear him out. I reached down deep to find the nerve to tell him.

"Dalog?" I asked, grabbing his attention.

He looked up at me.

"You've seen these creatures, right? I mean, obviously, you have seen them, but I just wanted to make sure," I asked.

I almost fumbled through my own words. Dalog extended his hand out. I reached out and grabbed it as if to shake it. He quickly drew his hand back.

"I don't want to hold your damn hand! I want the stupid holster. What am I supposed to do, hold this in my hand all day?" He snapped.

It made sense. I removed the pistol belt I was wearing and took the pistol holster from my vest. It doubled as a belt rig as well, thankfully.

"Why do you ask about these things? Yeah, I've seen em. Nasty fuckers too," he grunted out as he fastened the belt to his body, "Likely some Skinwalkers or even a ghoul. Have they started eating faces yet?"

My mouth dropped open at the thought. *Christ, I hoped they didn't eat faces.* This only added to the horror factor based on what I had already seen.

"You talking about those types of monsters from that game you like? Those creatures that lived beneath the subway line?" I asked jokingly.

"Hell no man, those are just regular cryptids. Get your head in the game, bro. I'm talking Skinwalkers. You know, like the Native American stories talk about. But there are different names for these ghouls or whatever they are all over the world," Dalog explained.

As he gave his best expert opinion based on lore, video games, and pop culture, X and Martinez joined us.

"Great! Another person. Glad to see you survived, Dalog," said Martinez.

Dalog sighed.

"Great. By movie logic, you just got me killed. But good to see you too."

I nodded in agreement. I felt that we've already used up our lifelines as it is. We shouldn't tread so lightly with passive phrases from the horror scene.

"How the hell did you make it here? It took everything we had to make it to the gym," X interrogated.

"Well, you see. What had happened was, I happened to find myself in the gym already. So, you see how this ends up. Me lifting weights, people dying around me. Of course I found somewhere to hide. I'm not about dying at this moment."

His explanation seemed legit. His shift started in the early morning, so he could have easily been at the gym this early. I occasionally ran into him on my shift early in the mornings at the gym.

"We're going for the Base Exchange," X said.

"Makes sense, that's where they're holding up the food and water. Oh, and not to mention the other things we could totally use to survive. But that's like two miles away. We shooting our way there?" Dalog asked.

Hell, I didn't stop to think about the second half of this journey. *How the hell were we getting there?* The thought ran across my mind a few times. I instinctively reached down into my vest pouches and drew out the remaining magazines. I think Martinez and X had the same thinking as they mimicked my moves.

"I got maybe two mags and some change left after earlier," Martinez said.

"I have another belt for the 249, but otherwise I'm almost out of 5.56 rounds," chimed in X.

"I'm down a weapon and have only three mags left," I said, doing the math in my head to assess the rounds.

"Yo, for real? Do you actually have a second M4 strapped to your ass, X?" Dalog asked while pointing to the second rifle X wielded, "Gimme the bigger one. I don't want this little pea shooter."

X hesitantly gave over the extra M4 she had taken from the armory.

Dalog checked it and loaded a magazine into it.

"So, what now?" Dalog asked.

I shrugged. I honestly was hoping to ride on the coattails of X and her quick thinking.

"I'm beat. My body is sore, and I'm exhausted. Hungry too, now that I'm thinking about it," Martinez said, moving to sit down on a bleacher seat.

Now that he mentioned it, I'm pretty exhausted too. Between feeling tired to start the day, not having lunch, and all of the excitement burning adrenaline through my body, everything caught up to me all at once. This was the first moment we had to just sit and breathe. The first moment, at least, since SGT Matthews. I remembered what I needed to do.

"Hey brother, I gotta tell you something," I began, "SGT Matthews didn't make it."

"Fuck," Dalog uttered under his breath, his smile erasing from his face.

"Another thing. Dude, Studds didn't make it either," I said trying to get the words out of my face.

Dalog sat down on the bleacher seat above Martinez. He sat back, letting his elbows hold his weight on the upper level above him. His face was emotionless and blank. It was apparent he was processing everything. No one dared say a word. We all knew we had time to process what we had witnessed back there. We grieved, or at least what could be considered grieving.

"Fuck," Dalog said, sitting up from the bleachers.

He looked visibly startled, but at the same time knew mentally that we all had to charge forward. One of the things they teach you is how to be numb to loss until the mission is complete. It keeps your head in the game. He let out a large breath of air from his lungs. He stood up from his seat, hyperventilating a bit. He flexed his arms a few times and cracked his neck.

"Well, fuck it. I'm not going to let these Skeeter Creatures get away with it, and turn all my friends all fuckerloo," Dalog grumbled.

"Skitter Critters," I corrected.

"Whatever. We need a better name than that. I'm digging Skinwalker right now. So, we are calling them that," Dalog asserted as he checked his newly acquired rifle out.

"Our end game is the BX. It's our best choice right now. Food and supplies will be overflowing there," X said as she made her way towards the exit doors.

Exhaustion must have taken over Martinez. He was passed out asleep where he sat. I took note of my own fatigue, as well. We would technically be getting off shift right about now. My muscles were on fire from the physical activity from the morning prior and I'm sure that the most recent festivities hadn't done me any favors. I opted to speak out.

"Yo, X. Is there a chance that we might be able to catch a quick nap for an hour? We already lost Martinez, and it would be a shame to wake him up," I said.

She thought about it for a moment. Maybe it was my bringing up the fact that triggered it. She looked like she was more tired than ever. "I'm willing to pull guard for about an hour if you guys need to. I haven't been awake too long," Dalog said.

X shrugged at the thought. She slowly made her way up to the second from the top step of the bleachers and settled down.

"One hour. One hour and we have to go. It's daylight so these things may not be as active," X said.

It made sense to me. I tossed PFC Dalog one of my magazines to ensure he had enough rounds if something went down. He now had the one already loaded in and my extra. He tucked it into his elastic waistband on his black shorts. I slouched onto the floor, resting against the lowest step. I figured it best to at least spread out to some degree. Dalog took one patrol around the perimeter of the room. It was full of weight lifting machines and treadmills. There wasn't anything we could use that felt useful. Dalog managed to make use of a few forty-five-pound bench weights and placed two or three against the entry door. Good thinking.

# Chapter 7

*FOB Centurion, IZ*
*0730 Local*
*February 12, 2010*

I lost consciousness sometime after Dalog dumped the weights against the door. I felt stiff. Sleeping in a seated position was not the best idea in hindsight. Dalog was sitting down on one of the bench press machines. I looked around to see who else was up and about. X was up and taking a few high-knee sprints against the far wall. I noticed her doing a lot of stretches too. It was probably a good idea to get the blood flowing, and everything limbered up. I took off my vest and helmet and cracked just about every joint I had in my body. Everything creaked and popped. My back popped audibly enough that it woke Martinez from his deep sleep.

"Jesus man, you over there crushing bubble wrap in your ass, B?" He groggily asked.

I smiled.

"Nah man. Fucking stiff as a board. How are you feeling?" I asked him.

"Can't complain," Martinez responded, stretching his arms while standing to his feet.

"Sure you can. I do it all the time."

"I'm aware, Holmes," Martinez laughed as he descended from the bleachers to the ground.

His boots were loud and heavy, banging with an echoing sound as he stepped down. I hoped the hell the creatures didn't hear that.

"We getting this food wagon moving or what?" Dalog asked, standing by the exit door.

He had already moved the weights away from the door. I guess it was time to leave the safety of the gym. After a few days in this place, it would likely become our tomb rather than a sanctuary.

"So, wait. Are we just going to go directly to the BX? That's still a ways away," I asked.

X shrugged. She chewed on the idea for a moment before coming up with an answer.

"Let's hit The Village first. It's like a maze in there, but we would be less exposed," she commanded once more.

"Great, sounds like a plan. I love this plan. I'm a huge fan of it!" I said sarcastically.

"Easy there, Venkman. The Village is our best bet. Plus, I can swing through and pick up pants. I'd kill for some pockets. Literally," Dalog said.

The four of us were on the move. Martinez slid the door open and peered down the hallway. It seemed like the chains on the exterior doors held by the looks of it. We four shuffled down the hall, lining up tactically behind SPC Martinez as he removed the twisted chains from the door handles. He passed the chains back through our line. X placed them down gently behind her and resumed her tactical position. We were ready.

The door creaked open, daylight flooding the entire hallway. It was bright out. It must have been about eight or nine in the morning considering the sun was directly in front of us. I left my watch back at the headquarters. A rookie mistake in the monster apocalypse I'd assume. Before I could say I was ready, Martinez and Dalog had already moved into position behind the first barricade in front of the gym doors. We decided subconsciously to move in pairs.

X and I followed just behind the other pair. We had a good hundred or so meters to go before the next bit of cover. Otherwise, it was a straight shot to The Village. I kept my head on a swivel. I looked just about every direction my eyes could reach. It was already starting to get hot outside. I was honestly hoping these things hated the heat too. I didn't see one in sight.

We continued to move down the road following the concrete Jersey barriers. The group halted underneath one of the giant concrete barricades, just outside of The Village. We were so damn close, why did Martinez stop the traffic? Up ahead in the distance, I saw it. It wasn't like the ones we had seen last night. At least, I couldn't tell what I was looking at entirely the previous night, so this very well could have been the same damn thing.

"Skinwalker, bro," Dalog said, poking me on the shoulder and pointing in its direction.

I saw it. We all saw it. None of us wanted to risk another firefight either. We knew last time, we rang the dinner bell and they swarmed us. This could also be a game-changer being in the daylight, however.

This creature was still dark in color. It was almost a brown-ish blue in tint. Maybe I couldn't see the colors in the dark. It had a head, but I didn't see any eyes that I could tell. The head was human-sized, just a little bigger than the average person's head. On its arms were giant claws. They were more like knife fingers, but I suppose they would constitute as claws in a biological sense. The legs were freakishly long, probably designed for jumping at us. I could make out small hands or arms on its chest area, like a bug. This thing didn't look like a bug, though. Maybe it was an alien bug. I've seen those movies before.

"What's the plan? Rush it?" X said, checking the chamber of her rifle to ensure the round was chambered.

"I say we sneak by. Best chance we have. We don't piss off the horde," I replied.

Martinez nodded in agreement. Dalog shrugged his shoulders. It seemed we were all in line to get past this thing. We hunkered down as low as possible. It was standing on top of one of the barriers that surrounded The Village. With luck, we could creep right past it without notice. I still didn't feel good about this plan.

"Low and quiet. Hold your shit, so it doesn't clank," X said, gripping all of the gear that dangled from her.

We crept in a crouched position slowly toward the entrance of The Village. So far, we remained undetected. I liked how this was going, considering the last night was an entire shit-show. I was worried about the fact we hadn't run into any other soldiers. Did they not have a chance? Were they all cornered and didn't make it? Or maybe they did make it and already evacuated, and we missed the memo. I had questions that needed to be answered.

We were only a few meters away from the opening that led into the housing area. This also meant we weren't far from the Skitter Critter up ahead on our right. Dalog gripped my bicep hard, a signal to stop in a formation. I reached forward and gripped X's arm just the same. She followed my direction and did the same to Martinez. We all came to a halt. Martinez looked back at the team. Dalog pointed to his eyes, then pointed off to our right. Our gaze followed his hand. Son of a bitch, there was another one of these things.

"Skitter Critter," I whispered.

"Skinwalker," Dalog corrected.

"Whatever. Plans?"

Dalog shrugged. We each looked around for a different route. We had anticipated getting around the one, but I don't think we had a backup plan for the second. It hadn't seen us yet, which was good. I had no idea what we were going to do.

"Better get an idea, it's looking at us, B," Martinez huffed out.

It was true. The ground Critter was eyeing us up. This one had two small antennae on its head and a yellow streaking through its body. Did they come in every color of the rainbow? Did we have to collect the whole set? I wondered what the colors meant. I didn't have time to really ponder the color spectrum, however, because Mellow Yellow Critter came at us.

This garnered the attention of the Blue Meanie on the barricades, and it joined the ranks on the ground with Mellow Yellow. I heard safety switches switch from safe to semi. I decided to do the same. They hadn't lunged at us yet, but I knew the moment was coming. Right on cue, the pair crouched down and began racing toward us. They switched between all fours to a more bi-pedal like stance. What the hell were these things?

On my right from down the dusty dirt road, I heard a loud roar. I was not prepared to deal with whatever lay just over the horizon. I retrained my attention to the Blue and Yellow pair of Skitters coming our way. All at once, the two stopped in the middle of the street, looking to their left, my right. They heard the noise too. Maybe it was their master?

The Skitters focused back on us but diverted their gaze between us and this mysterious growl. I was able to deduce that it may not have been one of their own based on Skitter body language. They picked the pace back up and clawed their way across the ground toward our direction.

Bounding at us, meters away, Critters descended on us. I raised my rifle and looked down the sights. I didn't want to fire off unnecessary rounds if we didn't have to. I wanted one or two shots to count. The roar became deafening. The sound was more of a machine sound, polluting the air with its roar.

All at once, I saw it. It came into my view as I prepared to squeeze off a round into the chest area of Mellow Yellow. The front of Dancer, the squad Humvee, slammed into both critters with a massive thud. Green-ish purple blood sprayed every direction. It was beautiful and disgusting at the same time. The vehicle drifted forward and slammed into the barrier, coming to a stop.

The engine was smoking. The dust was flying. It was so hard to see who the hell just saved our asses just now. My squad lowered their weapons. *Who the hell is this guy?*

"Yo!" Martinez called out to the driver of the vehicle.

The dust started to clear a bit, and a towering figure stood clearly wearing full gear, rifle slung. As the visage became more evident, it was apparent we knew precisely who our hero of the day was.

"Captain Seeker! My man!" Dalog announced as he walked up to greet him.

As the dust began to settle, more figures emerged from beyond the cloud. It was a few more people from our unit. We were starting to win at the numbers game. I walked up and outstretched a hand to shake Captain Seeker's hand. I was relieved to see him.

From the dust emerged two others from our unit that I could now recognize. The shorter of the two, SPC Eriks. He held onto an M4 of his own. His helmet was a little blood-covered. Obviously, he had seen his share of chaos. Next to him was one of the civilian contractors, Mr. Jarrett. He was a short, stocky African American guy from Philly.

He always prided himself on his hometown, even today. He wore an Eagle's Jersey, jeans and combat boots. He seemed the least tactical but the most comfortable of all of us.

Mr. Jarrett wielded a handgun that he clearly seemed uncomfortable using. He clearly was not a contractor that had the luxury of being prior enlisted. Someone gave him a crash course on this M9 and sent him on his way. Everyone shook each other's hands and greeted one another. Morale just took a hard swing to high today.

With the Skitters now dead, we decided to discuss amongst ourselves our plan. Now that we had a more significant number of survivors, we were a bigger target. A bigger target, with more guns.

"So, where were you guys headed?" X asked the newcomers.

"Honestly, the plan was to take the Humvee and get the hell away from here, but the engine started to overheat around the same time we saw you guys cornered. We made an executive decision," Captain Seeker said.

"Well, we appreciate that decision," said Dalog.

"Who's in charge of your little gang here?" Asked Seeker.

X and I looked at each other. Technically I was senior to her and Martinez, but she had been taking charge this whole time.

"Chantry, you're ranking lead, yes?" Seeker asked.

I choked on my answer for a second before I mustered up a response.

"Sure. Yes, sir. I am," I reluctantly muttered.

"Excellent. What is the plan?"

"Our plan was to get to the Base Exchange and see what we can get there. We still have some ways to go, but it was a good hole up point before getting to the airfield or a decent vehicle to get out of here," I said confidently.

Where the hell did my take-charge attitude come from? I surprise myself sometimes.

"Sounds solid to me. If we cut through The Village, making our way to the DFAC, we could easily bounce from there over to the path that leads to the BX. Magnificent." Captain Seeker said, resting his hands on his rifle that was slung from his vest.

I had a solid plan? Maybe I should give myself more credit than I do. I never really had to be in charge before since SGT Matthews always did the majority of the legwork in the squad. I never really had the need to be the guy in charge. If you're going to find your take-charge attitude, it may as well be in a life-threatening combat situation.

"Well let's stop standing around with our dicks in our hands and let's get moving!" Dalog asserted, pushing past Captain Seeker, "I also need pants still."

We all nodded in agreeance that the plan was in motion. We moved as a larger group now through the entrance to The Village. The rows of containers-turned-house now looked ominous and foreboding. They already didn't look welcoming, to begin with. We started down the middle road that split the sides of the housing. Dalog lived on the furthest side to the left of our position. We figured that was a good target to shoot for. We moved out, scanning each side of the containers as we passed each one. We split up through the area, some of us taking the spaces between the containers and barricades on the left, others on the right. Those remaining took the main road. We didn't want anything to surprise us.

We passed row after row, making our way toward Dalog's living quarters. I just wanted this side quest to be over with, so we could get back to the primary mission. SPC Eriks put his hand up. He managed to be forward of our position, a dangerous position to be in. None of us had decent coverage on him, and I think he realized that. Apparently, so did the creature that saw him as well.

Before any of us could react, Eriks was gone. He was grabbed as swiftly as Studds was back at headquarters. This time, it was a red and black colored Critter. We tried to move in on his position, but these things were fast and strong. It had already bounced over a few barricades with Eriks in tow before any of us could get a line on it.

"Shit!" Martinez yelled.

"Keep it down. Eriks should have stayed behind," X said to Martinez.

We recovered and moved down the remaining two rows. As we rounded the corner, we saw the red and black Critter up ahead. It was sitting with its back to us, directly in front of Dalog's CHU. Of course, that is pretty convenient. Before any of us could react or plan to attack, Dalog rushed toward the creature. He tackled it with all of his body weight. We noticed that Eriks was on the ground in front of where the creature crouched.

Dalog reached for his weapon. It had been dropped in the confusion of the tackle. I noticed the look on his face. It was a look of fear, frustration, and anger. As Red swiped him, he dove down toward SPC Eriks' position. There was a knife housed on Eriks' vest. Dalog grabbed it and reared back, stabbing the creature in its chest. He repeated thrusting in the center of its chest. The beast let out a gurgled screech before silencing all at once. Dalog let the animal fall to the ground, dropping the knife to his side. There was creature juice everywhere. The blood was a strange mix of colors that resembled an oil spill over water. I could clearly see everything now. These things had to be alien.

Dalog shivered in disgust before opening the door to his room and walking inside, letting the door close behind him. We checked on Eriks, who was very much alive at this point. That's a relief because he had us worried for a moment. We sat him up against the barricade and waited for Dalog to change. After much shuffling and scuffling from behind the door, he emerged, dressed in his standard fatigues.

"I told you I'd fucking kill for some pants. You thought this was a game?" Dalog said as he adjusted his armored vest.

I smiled and shook my head at him. We helped Eriks to his feet after a solid twenty-minute rest. We had to keep moving. We had to get somewhere that there were more people.

# Chapter 8

*FOB Centurion, IZ*
*1400 Local*
*February 12, 2010*

We were slowed down. Dragging Eriks with us meant two of us had to hold him up for support. Thankfully Captain Seeker was a big enough guy and offered to help pull him along. He was never afraid to get his hands dirty, and I respected the hell out of that. We traversed the rest of the catacomb-like rows of The Village, making our way to the entrance on the far side. It was a straight shot from here to the Base Exchange. All we had to do was pass by the sewage treatment facility and through the generator field.

I always hated passing by the treatment facility. The air around it smelled like death and poop on a normal day. Mostly poop if I had to put my money on a specific stench. The recent events didn't do it any favors. We trudged on, looking around all sides to ensure that a surprise attack was not waiting for us over the hills. The heat wasn't doing us any favors, either. Even in February, it must have been pushing at least a hundred or so degrees. The hot sun cooked me inside of my protective armor plating, but I was not taking it off for anything. This did wonders for my attitude towards how the day was playing out.

We tightened up our formation as we began to move toward our first checkpoint. With Eriks in tow, we were much slower now. All of us decided it was best to put less distance between each other for safety reasons. I was overjoyed when my nose was struck by the stench of the treatment facility. The putrid air burned my nostrils as it wafted by. We were getting close.

As we walked to the chain-link perimeter fence of the sewage treatment plant, we stopped. Eriks was having apparent issues, and Captain Seeker set him down against the fence. His breathing had changed, that much was clear. X reached down and opened his vest. It didn't appear that anything was wrong. There wasn't any blood. At least no more than the rest of us had on our bodies. I stepped closer to him and took a knee, using my rifle to brace myself as I lowered. It was only then that I noticed it.

An ivy-like strain of discolored veins starting to protrude from his shirt collar. The beginnings of what looked like something far worse. "His shirt. Can we lift his shirt?" I asked, pointing to his neck.

Eriks was near unresponsive as we unzipped the ACU blouse and untucked the tan undershirt.

"Jesus Christo. Dios Mio," Martinez said, standing up to walk a few paces away as he blessed himself with the four points of the cross over his body .

Dalog also stepped off a bit. It was probably best to give this guy some room to breathe. There was no need to crowd the poor bastard. I scooted closer to him before I continued to lift his shirt. He was a chunky guy. We were greeted by a few moles, some belly hair and sweat under his shirt. X pulled out her pocket knife and handed it to me. I cut into his shirt without hesitation. It took a few swipes to get through the fabric, but once it got going, it cut through with ease. I passed the knife back to her.

"Hey, buddy. You ok? How are you feeling?" I asked.

I don't know why I asked such a stupid thing. It felt like the right thing to ask. It also felt incredibly useless.

"My chest is on fire. It hurts. Hurts to breathe. Burning," Eriks gasped out in between breaths.

He was sweating profusely. He always sweats heavily, but this was much more than usual. Dalog did his best to stand in the path of the sun, providing Eriks with as much shade as he could.

"Am I dying?" Eriks asked through his breaths.

"I'm ordering you not to die, Soldier," Captain Seeker said as he shot a smile to Eriks.

"Roger that, sir. Permission denial acknowledged," Eriks whispered, laughing a bit as he did.

His laughing turned into heavy coughing. I looked closer to the wound that was on his neck. It appeared to have originated on his neck, not his chest. The injury also seemed to be growing. I couldn't find any puncture marks or bite entry wounds. I ruled out vampires and zombie scenarios in my head as I continued to look. I was by no means a medic, but I know for damn sure veins aren't supposed to be a bright blue-purple hue and bulging from the skin.

"Should we cut him open," Martinez asked, "you know, to let the poison out or whatever?"

I didn't even know if it was poison. It sure as hell looked like it. The wound could also have been some kind of embryo in his chest, ready to pop. I've seen far too many movies.

"Can you move? I want to get away from the poop factory if possible," I asked Eriks as another tinge of stink waved through my nose hairs.

"I need water, so let's go," Eriks muttered as he motioned for help to stand.

We aided him to his feet as best we could. Captain Seeker resumed his position to help carry Eriks along. Martinez stepped up, supporting Eriks' left side. We had to get through this plant. I took point. I knew exactly why I took the lead this time; I wanted to get the hell away from this treatment facility.

We slowly moved through each of the giant metal vats that stirred waste for cleaning. It wasn't until I passed by the second vat that I noticed something.

"You guys hear that?" I asked, looking over my shoulder to X.

"No. I got nothing. What am I listening for?" She asked.

That was just it. There wasn't a sound. It was absolutely still out there. The poo pushing blenders weren't operating.

"Power's out," Martinez said as he brushed passed me.

It was good to know the power was dead, but it didn't help us in the middle of nowhere. I wished I had some sort of a filter for my face. The center of this complex was awful. I needed to get far from it, and never look back.

Pushing through the thick, rank air was hard. We finally came out on the other side of the gate of the treatment facility. A flat road lay before us, separating the treatment facility from the generator field. The generators were giant behemoths of machinery. This is what powered a good chunk of the base. Surrounding the area were giant signs warning passersby, short cutters, and anyone who felt so inclined to venture through that it was a dangerous area. High voltage signs littered the area. But it looked void of any life. I consider this to be a plus in my book. I rallied everyone up around the outside of the fence.

"It looks empty over there, B," Martinez said as he stood on his tiptoes to look into the generator mess.

I relaxed my body in frustration.

"There are some things you just don't say. 'I'll be right back,' 'hold my beer,' 'let's split up.' Those are just some of the basics," I said to Martinez.

"Yeah, Chantry is right. It's horror movie rules. Now you just filled the whole place with monsters," Dalog said.

Martinez let the air out of his teeth in retort. His body language said it all.

"This ain't no horror movie, B," Martinez scoffed.

Almost on time, a small group of the Skitter Critters came out into the open around the sea of generators. I could make out at least four to five of them from where I stood. These ones were slightly different. They were a little bigger and more substantial looking than the previous batches we've tussled with. Maybe they needed new names.

"Christ. Are those bigger ones?" Mr. Jarrett said, stepping forward.

He had been quiet most of the way through the sewage plant. He was right; however, these did look bigger. Significantly bigger. The size difference was as noticeable as your average guy next to a bodybuilder. Three times the size of the Skitters we've come across so far. There was something else that was exponentially unsettling as we looked on to the crowd. These new creatures didn't have the claw-like hands the standard ones had. These were entirely different, looking like arm cannons. My heart sank a bit at the sight.

"Fuck me sideways. You telling me they got gun arms now?" Dalog said as he began to raise his weapon.

I was too busy wondering precisely what they shot out of the cannon fists to notice that they started moving in our direction. They were much slower, but clearly posed more of a threat due to the blaster fists. The first one to the right raised its gun fist in our direction. A few crackles of lightning and sparks formed at the opening of its fist. It used its other hand to move similar to a gorilla. These were clearly less agile.

"Scatter!" X yelled out as the blast of energy escaped the gun barrel knuckles of the creature.

We dove out of the way just in time as the energy ball cracked over our heads into the fence behind us. It didn't liquefy the metal links in the fence, so I assume that was a good sign.

"Again!" Captain Seeker yelled out.

We moved to separate sides of the road. We were now split several meters apart. What the hell were these things? I looked over at X, who dove to the left side opposite of me. I gave the signal with a head nod, and we stood up together. I flipped my weapon to hot and unload a few calculated rounds at the creature. As a matter of fact, it seemed everyone else in the squad received the memo as we all put a few rounds into big dumb and ugly. It lost its footing before being able to fire another shot off, hitting the rocky ground with a crunching thud.

We systematically moved on to the second one. There was no way to know what type of firepower these things required, but we also weren't taking any chances. One by one, we dropped the creatures as we ducked and weaved out of the way of each energy beam. The blasts were slow, not like bullets or anything I've ever seen. They were relatively easy to dodge if you saw one coming.

X and I moved forward. The last bastard was tucked away behind a generator, using its thick metal housing as a shield of sorts. Dalog followed us with Martinez shortly after. Captain Seeker and Mr. Jarrett stayed with Eriks. He didn't look like he was doing so hot. We needed to get moving. I fondled the trigger of my rifle with my index finger as we stepped through the warning fence. This was just some barbed wire someone set up to make it clear you shouldn't be here. They didn't do that good of a job of keeping us out. Martinez placed his boot onto the wire, allowing the rest of us to step over. I took point.

We scanned the rows of the generators. These monstrosities stood at least five feet tall at their smallest. They'd have to be massive if they're supposed to power this side of the base I guess. Row one was empty, save for a smoking carcass of beastie number one. Rows two and three were also void of life. I rounded the corner to check my nine o'clock, but it happened all too fast. I was face to face with this big nasty.

I was much too close for comfort. I could smell the stench of this creature. It had a bit of a musky smell to it as if a skunk died, was sprayed by a different skunk, then sprayed once more. It was potent, to say the least. It had two beady eyes at the front of its skull, which practically sat on its shoulders. It didn't appear to have a neck.

It had a set of jowls on its face. It reminded me of the Predator, except nowhere nearly as cool. Without hesitation or thinking, I jammed the barrel of my M4 into its over bitten jowls and squeezed the trigger. I closed my eyes and held my breath as a squeezed several rounds directly into the back of its skull, where I prayed its brain was housed.

A decorative spray of head matter spattered onto the generator body behind the monster.

"Suck my dick, you Big and Nasty!" I yelled out as the adrenaline coursed through my veins.

The monster slumped down into a seated position on its short legs. It let out one final gurgling breath before it let go. I felt like an absolute badass.

I turned around to rejoin the team. I noticed they were all staring at me in awe and disbelief. Dalog stepped forward and patted me on the shoulder.

"Hell of a catchphrase there, guy," He laughed.

*Catchphrase? What the heck was he even talking about?*

"All the action heroes have one. Arnie has 'I'll be back.' Bruce has 'Yippie Kay Ay.' You may have coined your action phrase," Dalog continued, "Just embrace it."

"My catchphrase, if I even needed one is not going to be yelling to 'suck my dick' to every creature I see. I don't need a catchphrase, either. In case you haven't noticed, we aren't exactly in a Hollywood blockbuster," I snorted back to him, wiping a few spats of creature blood off of my face.

Martinez stepped around from the generator and began to poke the carcass with his rifle.

"Ugly hombre isn't it?" He said as he poked the arm.

"You got a name for this one too, Chantry?" Dalog asked.

I hadn't given it much thought. I thought Skitter Critter was about the gist of what I'd have to use, naming convention-wise. Those were easy to call; they skittered, and they were critters. This thing was just big, ugly, and nasty.

"The Big and Nasty," I said proudly.

"I dig it. It's like the sandwich at McDonald's, but not. What if we called them Number 5's?" Dalog asked.

"Number 5's?" X asked. A puzzled look splashed across her face.

"Yeah. Number 5. It makes sense because that's what number it was on the menu board. Combo number 5. Call em Number 5's,"

I wasn't too keen on PFC Dalog's suggestion. I'd prefer not to be yelling out a number when it came to these things.

"Let's roll with Big and Nasty. Other people we come across might not get that name, and think we are saying there are five of these assholes coming for us," I asserted.

"Fair point," Dalog said, nodding.

We slugged our way back through the rock coated ground to regroup with Eriks and his care staff. Captain Seeker was standing guard while Mr. Jarrett knelt down to talk to Eriks. It was a sight that plainly indicated defeat, but in our eyes, we just kicked some ass.

"All clear!" X hollered to the trio, waving them on as she did.

The two picked up Eriks and began helping him through the generator field. We walked past several rows of generators once more. This time, however, they had a little repaint to the walls. Captain Seeker stared at the brain spatter coated walkway where I had my final showdown with the Big and Nasty. I glanced over to him at the right time because it looked like he was second from vomiting at the sight.

The other side of the generator field didn't hold any golden brick roads or a rainbow to a pot of gold. What we noticed on the other side of the large concrete barricade that protected it made all of our throats dry immediately. As we rounded the staggered barrier that prevented vehicles from entering, we saw the road ahead. Almost glowing like a beacon in the night, we saw the Base Exchange up ahead. It was a beautiful sight because it meant for us, the journey was over. We would have food, water, and other supplies and a good chance to figure our way out of this mess. Hopefully, other survivors were thinking the same. Captain Seeker adjusted his grip on Eriks, and we pushed on, heading down the flattened dirt path to the collection of shops and restaurants that surrounded the entrance of the BX known as The Carousel.

# Chapter 9

*FOB Centurion, IZ*
*1830 Local*
*February 12, 2010*

The sun was beginning to set by the time we made it to the entrance of The Carousel. I was thankful that the temperature was starting to wane off with every inch the sun fell in the sky.

The wind kicked up a little while we inspected our surroundings in The Carousel. Coffee shops, trinket stores, and burger shops encircled the area, closing us in. At the center of The Carousel was a giant stage, typically used when bands would do some sort of USO performance. We hadn't had someone come through in quite some time, now that I think about it.

"Hey! Eriks isn't doing so hot!" Martinez called to the group.

I looked back. It was true; Eriks didn't seem like he was the same color as he was before. The veins in his face and arms were now the purple-blue tint. It was clear that the wound from his chest was spreading. Was it a virus? Some sort of infection? I wish I knew more about what these things were.

"How are you feeling, guy?" Dalog asked Eriks, patting on his shoulder.

He didn't get out much more than a few unintelligible grunts. That was not a good sign by any of our standards. Captain Seeker took a knee, looking up at Eriks who was now supported solely by Mr. Jarrett.

"Listen, soldier. You need to keep going, you hear? I don't want you giving up. We just need to get you down that pathway and through the doors. You can do it. Hooah?" Captain Seeker commanded.

Eriks gave his best army "hooah" that he could grumble out and stepped forward to keep moving. He didn't look too good. He was sweating quite a lot and appeared physically weaker than ever before. I kept in the back of my mind, every movie I had ever seen involving zombies. He posed a clear and tangible threat if he mutated into a flesh-eating monster at any point. I dared not voice my concerns to the group. I didn't want to come off as entirely idiotic.

We picked ourselves up and made our way to the walkway of the Base Exchange. It was eerily quiet. I'd like to say the place felt still, but the wind was kicking up a bit. It was a sure sign a dust storm might be on the horizon. I crept up to the double doors that allowed entry into the massive steel structure. The sign on the front that illuminated the area with the soft blue glow of "BX" was no longer lit. That confirms that the Big and Nasty's must have siphoned the power somehow.

Aside from whipping winds whistling down the tunnel that was formed by barriers and building, it was silent. I peered into the window as best as I could, but it was pitch dark inside. The group followed behind me. It was evident that everyone was exhausted from the day. They routinely went through the motions to tactically stack on the door, ready to breach the building.

I took point for the breach. I held my hand out to signal the team to be ready. Slowly, I reached for the door handle and gave it a slight pull. It opened up with ease. Readying my rifle, I pulled the door open and stood against it. One by one, the team poured into the door. I could see flashlight beams shooting a stream of illumination into the room. The beams darting around frantically.

"Clear!" I heard SPC Martinez call out.

"Clear!" X echoed the command.

The main room had been free of threats, this was a good thing. I was safe to step in after helping escort Eriks inside. I closed the door behind me and flipped the latch to lock. It wasn't going to hold back much, but it was something.

I scanned the open room for any signs of life. It didn't even look like anyone had been here prior to us arriving. The shelves were intact and merchandise where it should be. But where was the staff? Had they been spooked off by whatever these things were? I pointed my flashlight beam across the room toward the tactical flashlight display. We were suckers for gear, and I wasn't immune to it either. It was the same brand I already owned, so I could vouch for its quality. I scooped a few of the clamshell packages out of the cardboard standee display and walked to the knife aisle.

I didn't pay much mind to the types of knives, I just needed the most accessible one to cut into the packaging. I saw a nice one that hung eye level; carbon steel blade, rubberized grip body. The grip was bright orange, you couldn't miss it. It was apparently endorsed by Bear Grylls, that survivalist guy that drinks elephant piss, so you know it's quality. I was able to rip the packaging off around the knife, allowing me to work at the thicker bits that housed the blade. After a few seconds of fuss, the knife came loose from the packaging. I figure it was meant as a deterrent for theft while employees were present, not while a soldier was ripping it off during the apocalypse.

The blade came with a beautiful canvas cloth holster for my belt. I tucked that away in my pocket to affix later when I had time. Scooping up the flashlight packages, I walked myself back to the team. Eriks was rested against the coffee counter. They weren't working but still had a good bit of water stacked nearby. Mr. Jarrett was looking at the magazine rack, thumbing through the latest sports magazine issue. Captain Seeker was making his rounds, checking on everyone that was inside. I saw X and Martinez loading up on protein bars and other grab-and-go food.

I dumped my loot onto the table just above Eriks' head. He didn't react to the clatter or the clack of a half dozen or so flashlight packages hitting the surface.

"Yo, if you don't have a flashlight, I got some," I called out to everyone as I began to cut the packaging away from each one.

They luckily came with a battery. Considering the price tag, they had better come with a damn battery. It's not like I paid for these, it was more the principle of the matter. I began unpackaging and loading batteries into the lights one by one. I stacked the lights face down onto the coffee counter. You could hear some of the crunches in the left-over sugar or other additives people left spilled on the countertop as the lights were placed.

I wasn't sure what else we could possibly need. I figured a handful of flashlights was a good start, as well as a knife. X walked over and placed a shopping basket full of granola bars and candy in front of me.

"Fuel for the road. At least they won't go bad," She laughed.

The bars she grabbed were the worst on the planet. But they were all we had, and she was right; they would keep forever. I wandered back over through some of the tactical gear aisles. I fished around for a few additional magazine holders, as well as a tactical rucksack. These things were great. They could hold so much gear but had straps that you could pull to tighten it to your body. It really helps with the rattle.

I picked out the slick black rucksack and made my way back to the coffee station. Mr. Jarrett was tending to Eriks. I didn't like the look on his face. I placed the bag down and stuffed it with a handful of snacks before heading over.

"How is he doing?" I croaked, the words barely escaping my throat.

"I ain't a doctor. What I can say is he ain't doing too hot," Mr. Jarrett said as he stood up.

He escorted me an aisle or two away before continuing.

"If he is gonna hold us back, I'm finna not be wit y'all," He said.

My face dropped. Was Jarrett suggesting we leave Eriks behind?

"Would you rather we left you here if this was you?" I hissed.

"Word. I ain't here to make nobodies time harder. I just want my paycheck, and to be able to fly home. If I was like him, I know I ain't collecting neither, feel me?" Jarrett said.

He had a point. I think he could see that I realized his point. My expression must have had that plastered all over it. But what the hell were we going to do with this poor guy? He's just a kid. Hell, most of us were. Aside from the Captain and Mr. Jarrett, I doubt any one of us was past twenty-five. Eriks wasn't even of drinking age. He hadn't had his first bar purchased beer, let alone the feeling of being with a woman far as I knew. There had to be a way to help him. I brushed past Mr. Jarrett and returned to Eriks. I rallied everyone up to join me.

"Ok. Here's the deal. We can't stay here, and that's obvious. We have rations and a few new materials, but that is by no means a substitute to get off this shithole. The base is clearly overrun, and we have to get elsewhere. Call in a bomb strike or something. I don't really know what to do in these circumstances," I commanded, "but what I do know is this; we have to get out of here."

The motivational speech must have resonated with the crew. I was met by several head nods of approval. I hoped the hell I was making sense because I had no clue what I was even doing at this point. I realized then and now that the entire United States Army was run this way. We were all literally making it up as we went. I guess it takes shit hitting the fan to realize the truth.

I looked around at the group as if fishing for advice on the next step. Everyone had looks on their faces as blank as my own. I couldn't get a read on anyone. Even though we were in a gold mine of material possessions, they all meant nothing if we couldn't live to use them. I tried to think of the best way to get off this rock. It was nightfall already. These things seemed to be more active at night. I'm not sure if it was the heat or the actual daylight that kept them at bay. I didn't want to stick around too long to find out either.

"Let's stick around here for the night," I said to the group, "It's the best option we have. We don't know how many of these creatures are running around the base."

Martinez nodded in agreement. X said nothing. I knew we would have to pull guard duty through the night. I decided to opt-in for the first watch. I assigned everyone a time to guard the place. After instructions were laid out, everyone went to a respective area to sleep. Martinez elected to sleep under one of the cash registers stands. It enclosed him on two sides, so I could understand the feeling of safety. Mr. Jarrett found a beautiful corner to post up in. He had apparently acquired a pack of Black & Mild cigars and was in the process of lighting one of them up. Captain Seeker was resting across from Eriks, who still lay up against the coffee station. Dalog splayed out on the floor in front of the magazine rack. I grabbed a stool from behind one of the cashier's stands and sat across from the main door. There was only one way in and out, making it easier to guard this place.

I watched over as everyone slept. It was eerily silent, save for the whipping winds outside. The stillness of the room was still unsettling to me. I kept feeling like something was going to pop out and get me at any moment. I heard a shuffling noise behind me. I whipped around

with my rifle and flashlight to see who or what it was. It was Eriks. He was standing up now. He shouldn't be standing up. He couldn't be standing up. And yet, there he was; standing on his own two feet. I got up off the stool and started over to greet him. Something felt off. I couldn't put my finger on it. It was just a feeling I had in my gut.

As I got closer to Eriks, I noticed his skin was coated in the blue veins. His eyes were bloodshot, and he was more or less unresponsive. I shined the light directly in his face, and he didn't react. I know I'd have some words to say to someone who did that to me. I watched as he started walking toward the door slowly. It was clear he wasn't paying any attention to me, so I made a dash to Martinez. I kicked his boot, and he jumped awake. Before he could get out any insults to his slumber disturbance, he looked where I was pointing. Eriks was shuffling toward the main door. He grabbed his handgun and stood up next to me.

"How is he standing, B?" Martinez whispered.

"I don't know. Eriks just stood up and started walking," I responded.

I began creeping closer to Eriks. I had lowered my rifle and let it dangle from the sling. I remained cautious because I've seen my share of zombie flicks, but this was no zombie flick. This was real life. Martinez put a hand on my shoulder to let me know he was just behind me.

"Hey, Eriks, where you going?" I called out to him.

He didn't look back at me at all. He continued to shuffle his way to the door, his head lowered to the floor. It was almost as if he was sleepwalking, but I knew better than that. Any second now, he's going to turn around and try to bite our throats out in a bloodthirsty undead rage.

Eriks made it to the door, which was locked and latched from the inside. He didn't reach for the handle to open the door. Instead, he bumped his whole body into it. His body collided with the door in a rattling whump. It was loud enough to garner the attention of most of the sleeping room. I saw Captain Seeker stand up from his post, bewildered that Eriks had moved without him noticing. I watched as he bumped into the door with his body once more. It was as if he was being compelled to leave the room but lacked the cognitive brain operations to manipulate a door. Something flew over my head in Eriks' direction. Martinez had thrown a candy bar at him. It pinged off of his shoulder and slapped to the floor. Eriks didn't budge or flinch.

"What the –" Martinez cried out as his voice echoed through the building.

Everyone started to wake up to see what the commotion was about.

Dalog made his way over to our position.

"The fuck is he? A zombie?" He asked, placing his glasses onto his face.

"I honestly don't know. If Eriks was a zombie we wouldn't be having this conversation, would we?" I asked.

Dalog shrugged as Eriks bumped his body into the door once more. Everyone in the room had started waking up and wondering what was happening. I wish I had the answers for everyone. I was just as dumbfounded as they were.

"Is he trying to go somewhere?" X asked from across the room.

I turned around and faced the rest of the room. I was tired of hearing the same stupid questions getting asked over and over.

"Listen, if I knew, I'd tell you. Eriks got up and started smashing his face into the door. Congratulations, you now know as much as I do," I frustratingly belted out.

The door banged one more time. This time, however, the locks gave way. They weren't meant to barricade by any means; only hold off something trying to get in while we prepared. Eriks stumbled out into the cool Iraqi air as the wind whipped sand around. I walked over to the tactical gear once more. I grabbed some ballistic glasses and some balaclavas to protect against the dust and sand. I tossed the rest to the group, and they donned their own respective face protection. I could feel the curiosity with the group. We needed to see where Eriks was going.

# Chapter 10

*FOB Centurion, IZ*
*0030 Local*
*February 13, 2010*

Zero-Dark-Thirty. Typically I'd embrace the nighttime and enjoy myself. The last two nights have made that damn near impossible. I usually enjoyed my midnight strolls on the base, but this time, things were different. This time we were following Eriks to whatever was pulling him forward. He didn't seem to pose a threat to us at this point. We may as well figure out what's doing this to him.

It could very well be the thing that snaps him out of it. We packed everything we could into the rucksacks and gathered ourselves to leave. He was a few feet from the door, and it didn't seem like he was moving at a quick pace. I peered out of the door into the night sky. Nothing appeared ready to pounce on us. Taking the lead, I stepped out into the night. Eriks didn't follow a direct path. He seemed to walk like a drunk who spent too much money at the local bar and decided to walk home. I was worried about him. He was a good kid, I hope this was fixable.

Everyone fanned out behind me in a staggered formation. We kept Mr. Jarrett in the center, but he now held onto SPC Eriks' weapons. It was probably for the better that he had firepower than be completely useless. We made our way back into the Carousel area. I didn't like how much sand was blowing on me, but I hoped the creatures had mutual feelings.

Eriks didn't stop. He continued to push onward unfazed by the sand. My group, on the other hand, was chewing sand non-stop. I pushed onward down the trail to the center of the Carousel. Visibility was low as the sand began to kick up. I did my best to keep eyes on Eriks as he rounded a corner, disappearing out of view behind a tall Jersey barrier. We moved tactically toward the barrier. I peeked around it and saw Eriks blindly walking down the center of the road into the dust storm.

X brushed past me. I'm not sure why she decided to rush movement, but I wasn't about to regain my position as the leader. If she wanted to run the show, she very well could. We began a faster pace, tailing Eriks only by a few meters. Eyes were all over as we scanned sectors for hints of these creatures. The last thing I wanted was to be hit by a lightning blast from the Big and Nasty. Eriks wasn't headed to a particular structure I could think of. We were going the opposite way of the housing and other buildings. He was wandering toward the perimeter wall.

I still didn't see any signs of people outside. This really bugged me because I'd half expect to see corpses or signs of struggle. There is no way we were the only ones to survive this thing. I bet we likely missed an evac of sorts. That makes sense. We continued to tail Eriks as he made his way to the gated checkpoint entrance just west of our location. He walked past each barrier and barbed wire fence without care. I was positive he scraped a large part of his arm against the wire.

Eriks took off at a dead sprint toward the Iraqi city we neighbored. I never saw him run this hard in his life, to be honest. He didn't struggle or stop at any point. I looked back at the rest of the group, and they mirrored my expression. X took off after him.

"Following?" I asked the group.

I received a shrug from Dalog and Martinez as they double-timed it behind X. Mr. Jarrett and Captain Seeker decided to bring up the rear. I figured the best option we had was to find out exactly where he was headed. The sand was thick, and the air felt thicker. Trudging through the sand was already a tough feat, and a sandstorm didn't make the journey any easier.

X kept her eyes focused on Eriks as we crossed the sea of sand. We all held our eyes on the man in front of us to ensure we didn't lose track of direction. That was where we had gone wrong. I should have known better to keep an eye out on our surroundings. Out of the sand and shadows emerged a Skitter Critter. It was already airborne before any of us could react. It landed directly on Captain Seeker, claw blades sinking into his shoulders. I turned and raised my rifle to engage. Dalog did the same. We unloaded a few rounds into the creature as it scuttled away in the sand. For an awkward body, these things were impressive on the sand. I think one or two of my rounds hit the creature in the side. It stopped as if reacting to the bullet. To our horror, the Skitter began to use its smaller claw to cut open Captain Seeker. He cried out for us to aid him. It was heart-wrenching to see such a large man of his stature brought down so quickly.

The Critter kept moving backward. It pierced Seekers' skin once more as it took more steps away from Dalog and I. Bullets rang out from my right, causing Captain Seekers' body to convulse and go limp.

"It's a trap, B. It was fucking with us. I'd expect any of you to do the same for me if they get me," Martinez commanded.

"True. I don't want to get cuffed by an alien creature from Jupiter," Dalog said as he lowered his weapon.

The three of us looked at each other for a moment. We understood what just happened and why. There was no way he would have walked away from this. If he did, chances are he'd be just like Eriks and be a mindless zombie.

I just realized we forgot about our braindead buddy. I looked back to see X crossing another large sand dune in pursuit of Eriks. This kid had endurance and stamina, something X was running out of quickly, I'm sure. She managed to disappear out of sight over a sand dune, headed toward the city. Nothing else charged our direction for a few moments. We agreed that we were in the clear by lowering our weapons to our sides.

"We have to grab X! She is following Eriks into the city!" Martinez growled as he started stomping through the sand in her direction. I'd swear if X were into dudes, they'd be a perfect couple. They'd spend the days trying to "out-macho" each other. He was right, however. We did have to get through the sand and find X. The sandstorm was slowly dying down but didn't go away enough to give full visibility. Dalog, Mr. Jarrett, and I followed Martinez through the hot sands of the Iraq desert.

I knew in my mind that it was a useless cause to hunt either of those two down, but it didn't deter me from pushing on. I think we all felt that way. We had to at least try. I could start to make out the outskirts of the city. It was surrounded by a few mud huts and shanty homes. I assumed these were people that wanted the suburban-style life at minimum cost. I didn't get it, but I didn't have to either.

Martinez stopped short of the broken wooden fence that surrounded the closest hut. Judging from its size outside, it couldn't have more than one or two rooms inside. I could almost tell what Martinez was thinking; he wanted to find a survivor. In a way, so did I. We hadn't seen anyone outside our little group since Captain Seeker showed up. I ran the numbers in my head, and the result wasn't good. Since this whole ordeal started, I've lost four or five brothers and sisters at this point. I tried not to dwell on that fact and have it cloud my mind and judgment. We were about to kick in a door to a local home, and I needed to be level headed.

Dalog stood on the left side of the door, and I followed behind him. Martinez placed himself at the front of the entrance to kick it in on the mark. Mr. Jarret found himself crouched behind a hollowed-out pickup truck that was left gutted and rusting in the yard. Dalog gave a thumbs up, and Martinez made his move. He gave one solid thrust kick at the wooden door, and it gave in. It folded on itself under the force and collapsed to the ground with a loud clack. It wasn't that strong of a door, to be honest.

Dalog moved inside with his rifle at the ready. Martinez was just behind. I went in but held my position at the door to keep an eye on Mr. Jarrett. He wasn't designed for combat, and I don't even know if he'd fired a weapon before. I couldn't chance him getting taken along with the others. The sand had dissipated enough to make out some of the night skies. Just moments ago, the sky was a red haze coated with small grains of sand. The air felt clear enough to breathe freely once more. I removed my face covering and put the goggles into my pocket. I heard a sound ring out from the hut.

"Clear!"

"Clear!" Martinez echoed Dalog's statement.

How is there nobody in this house? Truth be told, it was probably abandoned before the shit hit the fan. I felt like we should just push forward to make it to the city at this point. Martinez came out, holding his helmet under his arm.

"Holmes, I don't even know why there's nobody. It's freaking me out for real," Martinez said as he massaged his bald head.

"I'm glad I wasn't the only one thinking this," I replied as I laughed.

"Classic apocalyptic scenario. You got your big baddies. Check. You got a wasteland environment. Check. Absolute badass main characters that are totally killing it right now?" Dalog started.

"Check?" Martinez said, "There's at least one badass here. You guys are supporting. And it's not a damn video game, B! Get that out of your head."

I had to admit, our scenario did fit the bill for half of the video games I played back in the late 90s. Those were games, and this was life. So far, Dalog has had decent logic. The only issue I had with it was that it's a cliché thought process that followed pop culture, which in turn, followed patterns of real life. Video games and movies were always inspired by some real-life conventional thinking. I can't deny the fact that us being the heroic figures in the latest shoot-em-up game wasn't cool.

Martinez sat against the truck next to Mr. Jarret and began making small talk. He had the right idea; this was a solid spot to rest before continuing. We were already at least ten to fifteen minutes behind X and Eriks, which could be the difference between several miles and a handful of buildings at this point.

I felt it best to get our sorry asses in gear. We had sat around for enough time and couldn't waste another moment. Everyone seemed appreciative of the fact they got to get off their feet for a moment after trudging through the sands at least. I was given a few moments to shake the dust out of my boots, giving me a boost in morale as well. The path ahead was still dark, but we could see clearly now that the dust had settled. There was still a fine haze that filled the air, but it was tolerable.

I moved forward to the edge of the property line of the mud hut. I squinted hard, peering into the abyss of the city ahead. I couldn't see anything moving, but then again, I wasn't equipped with super sight abilities. We weren't too far from the city. I was positive we could be at the mouth of the main road that put us in city limits within the hour if we moved carefully. I motioned to the crew to saddle up, and we began a march toward the city.

The four of us huddled a bit too close for my liking. I allowed it because I had already seen what happens if we get too far apart. These Skitter Critter assholes preyed on stragglers. It was almost animalistic. I could swear I saw something like this on Animal Planet with lions and wounded animals. Dalog double-stepped it to catch up to my position.

"Hey, man. I got a question, so hear me out. What the hell is the plan, guy?" Dalog asked.

I kept my head facing forward and shrugged. I hadn't actually formulated a solid plan.

"I dunno. I figured we go to town to start. Do what we can to look for X for a while, and if that fails, regroup to develop a better plan," I said.

Dalog smiled smugly. "Sounds like a plan!"

I shrugged and quickened my pace. I wanted to find X and Eriks. Honestly, I was harder pressed to find X than Eriks because I knew she was at least able to fight. Eriks was already zombified at this point, and I didn't know what the hell was going to snap him out of it. Dalog dropped back a bit to join the tight huddle of Mr. Jarrett. We had to protect him at all costs. It felt like the right thing to do.

As we approached the trash-filled main streets of the city of Yawm Jayid, our pace slowed. The first thing I noticed was the stench. I always hated living in this country during deployment because of all of the smells, but this was new. It smelled of death. Had everyone been slaughtered here before we got to town?

We approached the first tall building. The rooftops weren't nearly as high as the buildings back home, but they tried. The building we took shelter beside was a four-story building, a skyscraper by their standards in this small village sized city.

"Ok, here's the plan. We are going to zig-zag up the road, poking into any building that looks like it's been breached by a person lately. It makes sense to look at ones that aren't obviously barricaded. We do not split up or separate under any circumstances. Copasetic?" I ordered at a whisper.

"Copasetic," Dalog replied.

I stepped out from the cover of the large stone building. The city was too quiet. On a typical night, it would be rather quiet due to the curfew placed by us, but this felt different. It was as if there was no life to be found within the city limits that housed a few thousand people. We moved along the side of the building toward the door. I reached for the handle, and It resisted turning.

"Locked," I sighed.

We continued our journey as planned to the two-story building across the street. Wading our boots through mounds of trash, we were careful not to crunch too loudly as to not tip off a Critter of our arrival. The road was vast. I never understood why they built their cities so haphazardly. Some streets wide, while there were others too narrow to fit a car into. I wanted to speak to the city planner about my complaint.

As my head was wrapped around memories of playing Sim City and my understanding of infrastructure, I hadn't been paying attention. As we neared the building, just a few meters from the side of it, a loud bang came echoing across the desert night air. Dalog thrust forward and tackled me to the ground with a thud. Before I could snap at him, I realized what he had done. The rocky face of the building was still crumbling from the impact of a bullet that pierced the side of it. Mr. Jarrett already had the right idea by crawling low to the side of the building for cover. Dalog and I did the same just before another round clashed with the stucco-like facing of the building we sought shelter behind.

# Chapter 11

*Yawm Jayid, IZ*
*0430 Local*
*February 13, 2010*

Who the hell was shooting at us? Did these stupid monsters learn to use guns now? I kept running scenarios through my head of a new type of creature that used our own technology against us. The rounds were well placed, however. I doubt any of these monsters could shoot worth a damn.

"Who the fuck is shooting at us?" Martinez said through his teeth.

I wish I had an answer. I grabbed a handful of rocks and pitched them into the street. A bullet cracked out of the barrel of a gun, striking the ground nearby where the building material fell. Whoever it was had their sights trained on us but didn't move from their position. It had to be a lone gunman.

"Single shooter probably. Not sure what kind of rounds are hitting the walls, so it's hard to tell if their friend or foe," I said to Dalog.

"Friend or foe? Dude. Do you not see them shooting at us right now? Are we in a different game server? Are you lagging?" He sarcastically asked.

"For the last time, it's not a video game. This is life. I would prefer to live, so what's the plan?" Mr. Jarrett stood up.

"I got a plan, but you won't like it," he said.

"You are not sacrificing yourself, sir," I said, standing up to meet his gaze.

I stared into his face long and hard. I didn't see any sign of bluffing. He was going to do it if I gave the word. I wasn't about to let him die for the two of us. There had to be another way.

I took a few moments to decide what we should do. If we sat here and waited out this guy, perhaps we could be seen better in daylight. If he'd seen the creatures, surely, he wouldn't want to kill a friendly force. Even if he was a Local National, we were now on the same side.

"Sneak around and come up behind the guy?" Dalog said as he grunted from standing up.

"Do you know where he is?"

"No, Chantry, I don't know where he is. Nor do I know who he is but it's the best idea I've got," Dalog snapped back at me.

It wasn't that bad of an idea. Maybe we could use the cover of the night to get closer. If we couldn't sneak up on him, we could at least get closer to be identified as human. One of us was going to have to stay behind to continue to draw fire.

"Ok, two of us go round back of this building and creep up a few streets. The other two will pitch small rocks out every minute or so to keep fire drawn. That also helps the other two determine a location with every shot. We close in and jump this guy, disarming him," I ordered, "after which we will talk some sense into this dickwagon and maybe we can all team up and save the day."

Dalog and Martinez nodded in agreement.

"Ok, so let's go ahead, and you take Mr. Jarrett, while Martinez and I chill here and throw rocks. The two of you go up and do the thing, and I'll distract them," Dalog said.

"Word. Just tell me what to do, and I got you," Mr. Jarrett said as he checked his weapon.

"Don't kill anything or make any unnecessary noises. Just let me take the lead and talk to whoever the hell is on the other end of this. Got it?"

Mr. Jarrett nodded and gave me a thumbs up.

The two of us left Dalog and Martinez behind as we rounded the side of the building. We crouched down and quickened our pace as we dashed from building to building. After we passed three buildings, I stopped. I waited for a sign from the other two that we were getting closer.

Right on cue, a gunshot rang out. We were much closer now. It came from a few more buildings up and probably about a street over. We continued our dash for another three buildings and halted once more. Bang! I could hear the sound was less echoed and more localized at this point.

I decided we would round the corner to take a look around. The two of us made our way to the edge of the street and peered around. I didn't see anyone in the street or sitting in a balcony. We must be too close. Maybe we were too far away. I had to wait for another round to fire.

Just like clockwork, the round fired. This time I was close enough to hear the brass hit the stone ground of a balcony above us. I motioned toward Mr. Jarrett in an upwards direction, and he smiled. He may not have been military, but he sure as hell had a solid understanding of things. I respected that about him.

The shot came from the building diagonal from us. There was a prominent staircase that led to the second floor, which had been barricaded. Clearly, the signs of a surviving human. I inched closer to the barricading work that was haphazardly thrown together. It was a collection of furniture and other household items that appeared to have been thrown down the stairs. I thought it best to find another way in.

I motioned for Mr. Jarrett to follow. We walked the perimeter of the building to scan for any means of entry. I found a window just around the corner that looked to be just the size of what we needed. I silently urged Mr. Jarrett to climb in while I assisted him. After he was inside, I hoisted myself up and into the room. It appeared to be some sort of bedroom at one point. It could have been a living room, it's honestly hard to tell with these people. The stairs that led to the upper floor and balcony were not blocked inside the home.

We moved silently toward the staircase. I motioned for Mr. Jarrett to wait for ten seconds before following me. I didn't want us both to be captured at the same time. I figured if we left a bit of an element of surprise, we would still have the upper hand. He gave me a nod of acknowledgment. I started up the stairs, weapon at the ready.

I stopped short of the top step. I felt it was best to not announce my presence all at once to this guy. I peered around the corner to see who was doing all this shooting. Before I could get a good look at the guy, another pair of hands grabbed me by the bulletproof IBA vest and threw me to the ground in the center of the balcony. I hit my head hard.

My head was still reeling from the bump I took as I tried to look around. I felt a knee in my sternum as if I was being pinned down. I could make out voices, but my brain was still trying to reboot.

"Who sent you? Unit, son! Call sign!" The voice screamed at me in a thick southern accent.

I blinked my eyes a few times, trying to regain my vision as best I could. I could see Mr. Jarrett slumped over in the corner of the rooftop. It would appear this is what being knocked out felt like. I didn't even know I was knocked out. How long was I out?

"Say again! Call sign! Unit designator!" The voice shrieked yet again.

Once my eyes stopped seeing triple of everything, I was finally able to focus. It was a large man with a bushy red beard. The sun had already started to come up, so I knew I must have been out for a while. I tried to sit up, but he thrust the knee into me harder.

"Who the fuck sent you, asshole?" The man said once more, this time sounding less patient than ever before.

"No. No one sent us. I'm U.S. Army. Specialist Jason Chantry from Virginia, U.S.A.," I croaked.

"That's better. Can't have folk just running up on us. Bad enough we got the bug fucks trying to suck out our brains, let alone some rogue Haji wanting to take on the world and kill us while our pants are down," Red Beard said.

He took his knee off my chest. He was a pretty big guy, and I could tell from the weight he put into me that he could hold his own in a fight.

"Name is Whelan. That's all you need to know. My friend over there, that's Jacobson. That's all you need to know. You and your friends will be fine."

"And that's all I need know?" I joked as I started to stand up.

Whelan shot me a look as he helped me to my feet. I still felt woozy from whatever hit me.

"So, anyone get the number of the freight train that hit me?" I asked, rubbing my head.

"That train has a name, and it's Rogers. He's the one who knocked you out. You make an awful lot of noise for some combat-trained fellers," Whelan said, lighting a cigar.

I hadn't noticed that they had Dalog and Martinez as well. Christ, we really didn't know what we were doing, did we? How did we even make it to this point? I decided to ask our captor rescuers precisely who they were.

"Ok, so you guys some mercenaries? Govie Contractors? What's your deal?" I asked, resting against the wall to stabilize myself.

"We are the guys you call when you need shit done," Jacobson said, taking a puff of his own cigar.

I saw the balcony was littered with bottles of locally sourced alcohol and cigar tips. These guys had either been here a while or really liked to drink. I wasn't one to judge. I decided to drag myself over to Dalog and Mr. Jarrett to check on them.

"Your friends are fine, they're sleeping," Rogers said in a thick New Yorker accent, kicking the heel of Dalog's boot, "Your Asian friend here but up a bit of a fight for all of two seconds, but he went down easily."

Rogers was a brick house of a human. He looked like he ate muscles for breakfast. His hair was cut short on the sides. He must have been a former Marine or something with the type of high-and-tight he was wearing. He was very tall too, which didn't help my fear of this monster of a human at all. Captain Seeker was a tall guy, but this guy would easily tower him by several extra inches.

"Who the hell sent y'all out here?" Whelan said as he sat down on a box to polish off his rifle.

I started to walk toward his location and leaned against the wall nearby. I didn't want to get too close considering I was just steamrolled into the ground only moments ago.

"Nobody, sir. Shit hit the fan on the base, and here we are," I answered, "we lost a lot of people. Good people."

I trailed off as I started to think of the names of the good guys we had lost. In less than a day, everyone I had known was gone. I still didn't even know what was going on with X. I noticed the other guys starting to come to.

"So, we were that easy to pick off, eh?" I asked sarcastically.

Whelan shot me a look.

"Fuckin Fobbits. Damn Pogues wanting to play soldier. You wouldn't know combat ops if it came up and bit you right on the dick," he grumbled.

Rogers came over and took a knee across from me.

"Listen, kid. I don't know what types of shit you've been dealing with up there on the base. All I know is we been having our asses handed to us by some flying bitch of a thing," he said as he rubbed the back of his neck.

Flying thing? I could tell my expression changed before I even uttered a sentence.

"Oh, you ain't seen the flying monsters snatching up all our boys?

What the hell are you flapping your gums about then?"

"No. We had some beasts with giant razors for hands. We called em Skitter Critters," I replied.

"Skitter Critters? Sounds easy to take down. We've been calling these assholes Ladybug from Hell, on account of their red wings with spots on em. Ladybug for short. Or Hellbug. Yeah, Hellbug sounds cooler," Whelan said as he stroked his chin.

I had to agree, our naming convention didn't sound as advanced either. At least we had that in common.

"Oh, we did hit some other kind of creature. Some big fat asshole that shoots lightning out of its fists. We called them the Big and Nasty," I said, remembering the encounter at the generator farms.

Whelan stood up and walked toward the balcony.

"Christ, there's more of them? I thought the flying assholes were more than plenty," he said as he peered over the balcony, "they won't come over into the city. They picked us off when our trucks broke down about two clicks up the road east."

The mere fact that there was a creature out there that had an advantage over us that we didn't, scared the shit out of me. It was bad enough that the Skitters could climb walls with ease. At least the fat ones could be outrun if need be, barring any strikes from the thunder balls. Flying monsters was a whole new beast. I started to mull the whole thing over for a few moments.

I noticed that Martinez and Dalog were both to their feet, more than likely demanding answers. I figured I should be the one to break the bad news to them.

"Hey, they're cool. These guys didn't trust us or know what our endgame was, so they brought us here. I don't blame 'em," I said to the rest of my gang.

Dalog didn't seem to care. Martinez, on the other hand, he was still a little upset that someone got the drop on him so easily. Mr. Jarrett stayed in the corner he was propped up in. Probably a good idea for him to steer clear of this freight train crew for the time being.

"So, who the fuck are you guys? I don't recall hearing that player two entered the game," Dalog said as he sneered at Rogers.

"Easy there, hotshot. No need to get put back in the ground. Rogers will be more than happy to demonstrate exactly how we took down your friend Chantry here," Whelan laughed.

Dalog didn't seem to find it funny.

"We got a plan or something? You guys don't seem to be doing much better than we are," I said to Whelan.

Whelan shrugged. He went over to a large green container and kicked the lid open with his foot.

"Planned on shooting our way out of here, actually," he said as he pulled a small box of ammunition from the container.

"I'm all about going full Commando up in here, but where are we heading?" Dalog asked.

"Well, we were headed to the base. Sounds like that might be a lost cause," Whelan lamented, "but I figure it might not be out of the cards just yet. You guys had vehicles, and we need wheels."

Back to the base? Was this guy nuts or something? We just shot, shit, and screamed our way to this point already and now we are going back?

"That just means the creatures are going to be harder on the way back. We've clearly leveled up, and now we do a speed run through familiar territory. It's lazy game writing, to be honest," Dalog said as he fastened his gear to himself.

"Your friend thinks this is a damn game?" Whelan bellowed.

Whelan walked over to Dalog and grabbed him by the vest.

"Now listen here, Sally. We ain't in no damn vidya game. We are losing good men and women every second we sit here on our thumbs and twirl, got me?" Whelan growled at Dalog, his face barely an inch from Dalog's.

Dalog nodded. Whelan let him go and walked back to his weapon.

"Saddle up, ladies! We are going on a road trip!" Whelan commanded to his group.

I decided that maybe having the muscle around wasn't such a bad thing. Whelan and his crew seemed to have a handle on what was going on and could probably outmaneuver us. Hell, these guys got the drop on us once and knew we were coming as it is. It was perhaps best to move out. We had to find X first, however.

"Hey, Whelan. I got a favor to ask, do you mind?" I asked, trying to get the words to come out.

"Shoot."

"One of our own, PFC Alexopoulos headed this way not too long before you guys ran into us. Have you seen her? She was with a big guy named Eriks," I asked.

"Damn. She still alive?" Whelan said.

"Hell yeah, she's still alive, B! We gotta get her!" Martinez interjected.

"Alright. Men! We gotta get through this city and find this little lady. She needs our help. We could use the extra gun as well. Once we get through, we head back to FOB Centurion and get off this prison from hell." Whelan ordered.

His men didn't say anything. They nodded as they grabbed their gear and began loading up. The big guy, Rogers, went over to the crate of rounds and tossed me a few boxes. They were 5.56 rounds and a lot of them. This was almost the same feeling I had when we loaded ourselves up in the armory room. I quickly helped pass out the ammo to my team. We made sure Mr. Jarrett had enough to get himself through as well.

"What's with the Civ?" Jacobson asked, pointing at Mr. Jarrett.

I looked over at him. He was fumbling with the rounds, trying his hardest to load the magazines he had on him.

"He did some support level work for our unit. He made it out with us and held it down since. He's good people," I said.

"Philly guy, eh?" Rogers jested.

"Word. Born and raised. Eagles have my heart," Mr. Jarrett said as he looked down at the Eagles jersey he wore.

"Well, I hope that whatever the hell this is, we take care of it. Be a shame for the world to end and Philly not win a Superbowl." Rogers laughed.

Everyone finished loading up and moved toward the exit of the building. It felt nice to actually get off our feet and relax for a few moments. Hell, it felt good to talk to different people again. We almost felt normal for once since this whole thing started. Once we made it to the city street, everyone took up a position for guard. I stood myself on the far end of the building, giving myself a line of sight down two roads.

"So, where do we start looking for your friend?" Whelan asked.

"I have no idea. She could be anywhere, so we should look for signs that X has opened a door or something," I said, wiping the sweat from under my helmet.

"Let's split up. Chantry, Myself, and Dalog on one squad. Rogers, Jarrett, Jacobson, and Martinez on the other squad. Good?" Whelan commanded.

"Copasetic," said Dalog.

The two teams split off to cover ground in the whole city. We needed to move through a hundred or so buildings looking for signs of life. I wasn't sure how long these guys were going to play hero, but I wanted to use every second I could to track down X. Dalog and Martinez must have felt the same way. She was one of us. We walked off around the corner, weapons at the ready in search of our lost soldier.

# Chapter 12

*Yawm Jayid, IZ*
*1230 Local*
*February 13, 2010*

The sun was directly over us as we walked through the city streets of Yawm Jayid. We looked for any sign of human life, particularly that of PFC Alexopoulos. I always assumed that it would take an entire army to take her down, not a possessed SPC Eriks. I never once gave up hope that she was still kicking somewhere. My search companions felt otherwise, however.

Whelan seemed to be a man on a mission while searching for

Alexopoulos. The problem is that we were on two separate tasks. He seemed to be going through the motions to track her down or at least kill enough time to appear that we did all we could. Dalog meandered behind a bit covering our six as Whelan, and myself cleared building after building searching for our lost battle buddy. The sun was scorching hot as it sat directly above us in the high noon hour. I was starting to come to the same terms Whelan and his crew came to when we announced she was missing. I was beginning to give up hope.

I used my rifle to ease myself to the ground, resting myself up against one of the buildings we just searched. I removed my helmet and tossed it into the sand beside me. The heat was overbearing, and I was losing hope by the second. Dalog wandered off a bit as he seemingly scouted around the area. I didn't care because I was overheated. I watched as Whelan whirled around the corner to clear the area. I guess he assumed if we were going to take a break, the space better be safe.

SPC Dalog was peering into some of the buildings across the way when I heard it. It was a flapping noise, following by a low guttural squeal. I looked up into the sky, blinded by the sun as I did. I couldn't see anything flying from what I could tell. The flapping noise became louder. Whelan doubled back to my location as I was standing to my feet, reattaching my helmet.

"Christ. It's one of them Hellbugs. Stay low and against the buildings," Whelan ordered.

I made eye contact with Dalog. He heard the sound as well. The flapping sounding like a beast of a creature was soaring overhead. It was similar to the sounds of what I'd expect a dinosaur to sound flying overhead. It was bigger than anything I'd ever seen flying overhead before. The shadow cast as it passed by was massive. I felt a chill run down my spine as the shadow went past at a high rate of speed. I could handle the ground-based creatures. I don't think I was mentally ready to face this flying son of a bitch. Once again, the shadow passed over us. It was big enough to block out the sun momentarily. The sound of its wings flapping, combined with the shriek of its death call were enough to get the biggest guy to turn tail. That was precisely what I planned to do. I wasn't the biggest guy out here, but I was damn sure the smartest to realize I needed to get inside a building and wait for this thing to fly off in search of better things.

Whelan grabbed me by the handle strap located on the back of my vest, pulling me back against the wall with a thud.

"The fuck you tryin to do, son? That thing'll pick ya off out in the open," Whelan barked.

I didn't think about the fact the tall buildings were actually providing some sort of shelter from this thing. I still hadn't actually seen it. The shadows overhead, as well as the sound, was more than enough for me. Dalog was pressed hard against the building across the street. His gaze was fixated on something above. I could see the look in his eyes that he could actually see the thing. He pointed slowly at the rooftop of the building Whelan and I were pressed against. I hesitantly raised my head to look toward the roof. As my eyes met with the midday sun, it blotted out quickly. The Hellbug dove down from the rooftop. Its trajectory directly aimed for Dalog.

"Fuck me! Fuck me! Fuck me!" Dalog screamed as he rolled out of the way. He pressed his body hard into a doorway. He gave me a look as if to tell me he was about to make a run for it to our side. I shook my head violently in protest of his stupid idea. This was suicide. He grabbed his helmet and strapped it on a little tighter as he started to his feet. He was going to do it. He was making a run across the wide-open street.

Dalog's boots thudded against the sand, stirring up dust with each heavy footstep. From where I stood, he ran in slow motion. He couldn't run fast enough. He paused in the middle of the street and looked over his shoulder upwards. Before he could do anything, the Hellbug swooped down in his direction. I got a good look at it this time: red wings, crimson like fire. They were very much like ladybug wings combined with a moth. The body looked like a grasshopper mixed with a bear. I don't know how else to describe it. It wasn't a thin body by any means. It was as if a bear sprouted wings and bug arms and took flight. Usually, beetles and other bugs had pincers or something for its face, but this was different. It had a muzzle like a dog. Hellbug about sums it up.

The Hellbug dove down with its claws outstretched for Dalog. I couldn't ready my weapon fast enough to save him. Whelan was too busy looking terrified to be useful. Whatever the hell these things did to his men, it seriously fucked him up. Bigtime. I was about to be on his level.

As Dalog dove face-first into the sand in a last-ditch effort to save his hide, bullets cracked out overhead. They were short bursts. Controlled bursts. They were the bullets from my least favorite weapon. Continued fire ripped through the air as the Hellbug screeched in anguish. The rounds were a direct hit to its torso. A green-ish colored slime oozed out of its core as it tried to fly off to safety. It failed to ascend correctly and slammed into the building Dalog was crouched against initially. It crashed into the building, knocking parts of the building off as it did. The Hellbug came crashing to the street in a loud thud, sliding across the sandy dirt road in a massive dust storm. I followed the carcass with my eyes as best I could through the cloud. As the body skidded to a halt, I noticed it fell short in front of two combat boots. The owner of the boots put three to five more rounds into the head of the beast, snuffing the lights out for good.

The dust began to settle after a few seconds. Dalog was covered in green bug blood, resting in a fetal position in the road. I looked back to the mystery Rambo who saved the day. It was Alexopoulos, posing as badass as she could, with her M249B resting on her shoulder. She had her ballistic sunglasses on and one of the facemasks we picked up
wrapped across her face, but I knew it was her.

"Get up, you baby!" she called over to Dalog.

He was already sitting up, wiping the goop away from his face.

"Christ, kid. Is this your friend we were going to rescue?" Whelan asked as he stood to his feet.

I nodded and smiled. I got to my feet and walked to X.

"Seems like we needed a damn hero around here!" I called to her.

X slung her weapon and extended her hand to help Dalog up. He accepted the assist and stood to his feet, still shaking bug guts off of him.

"When we get back to civilization, I need a shower, a smoke, and a shower. In that order. I feel like the floor of a taxi," Dalog said as he whipped more goo from his body by flailing his hands.

"Eriks?" I asked, getting right to the point.

"I followed him for a while. He didn't snap out of it. I tossed a rock or two in his direction, too. Nothing. He didn't even flinch, man. Like a damn zombie," X said, pulling down her balaclava.

"Patient Zero?" Dalog asked.

"Huh?"

Dalog approached X.

"Patient Zero. You know, the first infected. Think he is the start of the zombie apocalypse?" Dalog asserted.

X smiled.

"This is not science fiction, broham. Although, with flying bugs and shit, maybe it is. But Eriks wasn't a zombie," X started, "He was something like a zombie, but it was more mind control. He walked down to this cave a few clicks west of our position and went inside. I waited a few moments before following. You wouldn't believe the shit I saw."

Whelan's expression changed.

"What did you saw?" he asked.

"Hundreds of them. Maybe even more. They were all just standing there. It was creepy as shit," X said as she shuddered.

"Hundreds of what? Bugs? Zombies? Pokémon? Aliens? Can we get a lifeline? I'd like to phone a friend for this one, X," Dalog said. "People."

"People?" I asked, trying to clarify with X on what she saw.

"People. Hundreds of them. Wall to wall bodies," X said as she illustrated with her hands as if she saw it in front of her.

Christ. Was this for real? Were they just killing us and harvesting us? What was their end game? So many questions ran through my head with what X just told us. I was pissed off, scared, and confused. I wish we knew more about what was going on.

"What do you mean 'bodies'?" Whelan asked.

"They were still alive. The people were all just lined up, shoulder to shoulder. It was like they were in formation for something. Row after row of person, American and Iraqi alike."

"Equal opportunity zombie. I dig it," Dalog said as he dumped sand out of his left boot.

Whelan began moving to the edge of the building.

"We got your friend. Let's regroup with my boys and get the hell off this shit shack," he commanded as he rounded the corner.

I looked at X and Dalog. Dalog shrugged as he moved on to follow. I figured it best to hang back and explain to X who this guy was and what we were planning. I went on to fill X in on the details of our adventures since we separated. She seemed a little upset about Captain Seeker, but she kept moving. We've lost so many people already, not including the ones we haven't seen from our unit just yet.

Whelan put his fist up to halt us. The three of us stopped moving immediately. I readied my weapon, preparing for whatever may be up ahead. I was barely given any time before Whelan moved into action. He whipped around the corner before any of us could cover him. I heard a lot of commotion as I moved to the edge of the building. Rounding the corner, I witnessed one of the most macho moments I had ever seen in my entire life.

Whelan had Rogers by the throat, and Rogers by Whelan's. Both reacted faster physically than they could mentally, and I appreciated that to a degree. Once the two identified each other, they let go and laughed it off.

"Christ, I coulda killed ya," Whelan said.

Rogers nodded. Martinez lowered his weapon. He was clearly on edge from something. I can only assume it was the same Hellbug that flew overhead not long ago.

"You guys kill that thing? I heard gunfire," Rogers said.

"Nah. The girl did," Whelan said, as he pointed back toward X as she rounded the corner.

Martinez' entire expression changed. I noticed that Mr. Jarrett also had a bit of a smile on his face as he stepped out from behind Jacobson.

"I figured you were monster food, for real," Martinez said as he approached X, patting her hard on the shoulder.

"pssh. Yeah right. It will take more than that to bring me down," X's expression changed, "but Eriks on the other hand."

The group of us huddled against one of the storefronts in the main square. It had decent cover on each side, as well as the awning. There were only one or two ways at us, and I felt better discussing our situation in this location.

"What's with this Eriks dude? He AWOL?" Rogers asked, stroking his hand through his beard.

X leaned against a table that was covered in debris.

"No. I think he got bit. Maybe he was cut by one of these things. I really don't know. But he started acting funny after that," X said.

Whelan rested against a pillar that held the awning up as he drew a cigar from his chest pouch.

"Funny? Did he get all sweaty and sick lookin'?" Whelan asked, sparking up his cigar.

"Yeah! But he was always sweaty. We barely knew the difference until his veins-" Dalog started.

"turned a purple tint and grew up around his body, eh?" Rogers added, after cutting Dalog off.

"Yeah, that. Purple veins and stuff," Dalog muttered.

"Yer friends gone, kid. Tough break," Jacobson said as he kicked a stack of papers over that was laying by the doorway.

Whelan took one long drag of his cigar, bellowing out a massive cloud of smoke from his face. He rubbed his brow for a moment with his thumb and forefinger before he spoke.

"Guys. We lost a few men the same way. There's no getting them back. Once they go dead-eyed, they're done for. Trust me on this one," he said.

*Dead-eyed?* I thought to myself what the hell Whelan was even talking about. Like a zombie? I looked at Dalog and saw he had a similar look on his face. I wanted to tell him to drop the Hollywood ideas from his brain, but I couldn't help myself either. The ideas stuck in there. Playing over and over in my mind. Eriks had gone zombielike, true. But was he an actual zombie by textbook movie definition? He didn't eat our brains or start to decay. He looked more like he was mind-controlled.

I slung my weapon back over my shoulder and started for the street.

"You guys coming? X, you said you saw where Eriks went, right?" I called over my shoulder.

X nodded and stepped in front to take the lead. We spread out into a lethal-looking fighting force. Even Mr. Jarrett was learning the ropes a bit. Good thing we were fighting an enemy that didn't care what uniform you were wearing. An Eagles jersey sure as shit stuck out like a sore thumb amongst all of our desert camo colorings.

The lot of us began to move and cover down the city blocks toward the limits. X was taking us to the west side of the outskirts out town by the look of it. Whelan brought up my left flank. I have to say it felt good to have some guys that knew what the hell they were doing fighting with us. Not that we had a rough time getting where we were, but we weren't combat grunts by any means.

We reached the last building in town. The sprawling desert in front of us was ominous and foreboding. I wanted nothing more to do with sand after we got back home, that much I can assure you. X motioned for us to move forward once more. This time we were ready for whatever came our way. I scanned all of my sectors and ensured we would not get surprised again. Rogers was looking at the sky the whole time, clearly scanning for a Hellbug. I wasn't entirely sure I liked that name, but it sounded more kickass than a Skitter Critter. It started to grow on me after a while.

As we crossed several dunes in the hot Iraqi afternoon heat, X stopped. She motioned for us to halt as well. Each of us did so, guns trained on each direction.

"There. That's where Eriks went to," X whispered, pointing to some mine-like cave.

The cave entrance looked like they were digging for something inside.

Man modified, clearly. There were wood support structures on the outside of the cave. Lanterns were hung to each side of the entrance, as well as makeshift seating just to the side of the mouth of the cave.

"No. Absolutely not. I've seen this play out a million times in video games. This is where the final boss is. Uh-uh, nope," Dalog said as he started to turn away.

"Dude. Come on. It's not a video game or a movie. This is life, and we need to save our buddy. If he's in that cave, then dammit, I'm in that cave. Let's do this and get the hell out of this shithole of a country, brother," I said.

Martinez shot me a look. I think I surprised him more than I did myself with that motivational speech. It must have worked because we all started checking our weapons. I loaded a full magazine into the rifle and chambered a round. I wanted to know that I had a full fifteen going in. Dalog jumped up in down in place.

"This is nuts! This is nuts!" He recited over and over as he psyched himself up.

X cracked her neck and removed her weapon from safe to semi. I knew this was it. The group of us, two by two, descended into the entrance of the cave.

# Chapter 13

*Yawm Jayid, IZ*
*1400 Local*
*February 13, 2010*

The entrance of the mineshaft felt damp and gross. It was noticeably cooler after a few steps into the shaft. I was mildly relieved to be out of the heat, yet equally displeased that we were going into a dark, unknown cavern of sorts. The stench was the first thing to hit my senses. It smelled like rotting meat coupled with three-week-old urine. The cavern mouth lowered into a cavern full of twists and turns. I couldn't see too far ahead, only that it took an immediate left a few feet into the entrance.

X reached into her pouches on her vest and withdrew several chem light sticks. She must have been smarter than I was because I didn't think to grab anything like that while we were on our makeshift shopping spree. Whelan reached out and grabbed a stick and cracked it. He shook it until it glowed a bright yellow color. X took one and tossed it several feet ahead of us. It illuminated the corridor in a sickly, pale yellow glow. She tossed each of us a stick to wear on our bodies. "These things don't last forever, but Eriks wasn't too far into this tunnel. I don't think there is another way out other than this entrance," X said as she tossed a stick to Dalog, "make them last and make them count. I got enough to light our way too."

She did a quick headcount of how many sticks she had stashed away in her ammo pouches. It seemed like a dozen or two by my eyeballed count.

"What the fuck are we waitin' for?" Whelan asserted as he slapped Rogers on the back.

Rogers took point, weapon out. X followed shortly behind him, chem light tossing every so many steps we took. She waited until it was dark enough to require a stick, she wasn't stupid about it. Martinez brought up the rear with Jacobson, keeping Mr. Jarrett in the middle. It still felt our duty to protect the civilian, and it seemed that Whelan and his crew were on the same level.

About half a kilometer or so into the cavern, the air started to cool significantly. On the surface, it must have been around a hundred or so degrees, but down here a solid sixty degrees and cold. I glanced around to look at the rest of the team to see how they were doing. X was focused as ever, walking to the left of Whelan who had picked up the pace, just a few feet or so from Rogers who led the back. Behind me was Dalog, next to Mr. Jarrett. The rear was brought up by Martinez and

Jacobson. Nobody dared make small talk, the echoes of our voices would carry through these caverns like a loudspeaker and signal our arrival. I wanted to remain as quiet and stealthy as possible. If there was a Skitter or a Big and Nasty in here, I wanted to know before it knew about us.

The cavern came to a split. There were two forks, one to the left and the other to the right. Rogers put his hand up to halt us. Everyone huddled around each other to minimize noise pollution.

"Split, or pick a hole?" Whelan asked.

"That's what she said?" asked Dalog as he smiled.

Jacobson shook his head, as did Martinez.

"We got two choices. We stay together and waste time going down the wrong tunnel, or split up and split our numbers doing so," Whelan whispered.

"Shit. I'd rather not split up. But we would cover more ground by doing so. There's no way to signal to the other team that we've found something, so I'd vote for sticking together in one tunnel," I said.

Whelan looked at me and turned his mouth in acknowledgment. I actually was making sense, something I had never done in my four-year Army career thus far. I never would have dreamed of opting for being a decision-maker or an idea-giver. Then again, if you would have asked me a week ago if I'd be fighting bug monsters from Mars or something, I'd have laughed in your face. Here we were: monster hunters.

"Ok, so the coin flip: left, or right?" Whelan asked once again.

Hell, I didn't think about what the right answer was. I just wanted to get this moving meat wagon rolling towards its dinner destination at this point.

"Left," I said.

Whelan shrugged and pointed toward the leftmost entrance to the tunnels. Rogers nodded and started to enter the tunnel. The group of us followed behind him, ready for what could be around the next bend.

We had walked for what seemed like hours. I've always been told by my mother that if I didn't stop digging a hole in the backyard, I'd end up in China. This is a far bigger hole, and much further down. Where the heck would we even end up? The middle of an ocean? Geography wasn't my strong suit.

"Going into the hive, bro. I'm telling ya," Dalog whispered up to me.

We had now formed a single file line. The tunnels were narrowing more and more as we went on. X was still popping lights off every so often, so we could make out the tunnel and our bodies, at least. I really wished we could just turn around and get the hell out of here. I didn't belong in this heroic rescue mission at all. I'd rather be where

I should be, working in that dank, musty office for eighteen hours a day.

It surely sounded more appetizing than the certain death that waited for us down this trail. X popped yet another chem-light and threw it on the ground by our feet.

"Last one," she whispered back to us.

Well, that's reassuring. I'm looking forward to being in pitch darkness walking to a feeding frenzy. I could be walking to a 'boss fight' as Dalog has brought up a hundred times. I was hoping that we would just pop out at the other end, or someone would decide that we have taken the wrong tunnel. I'd prefer an uninterrupted retreat right about now. If Eriks is down this far, well, that's his new home now.

I slowed my pace a bit to adjust the straps on my helmet. I always hated wearing these things, but I'd prefer to not take a head injury if I could help it. As I yanked on the left side strap, the group ahead halted. My heart raced. What had they seen?

Quickly, the group pressed themselves against the far wall and hunkered down. Rogers saw something. I decided to creep my way to the front of the pack again and see what was going on. I passed by X and Whelan. Neither of them budged. Neither spoke a word. Whatever was up ahead was enough to shut the whole team up. I placed my hand on Rogers' shoulder. He jumped slightly as I did but looked over at me. Silently, he nodded in a gesture, forward in the two o'clock position. Just up ahead on our right was a bit of light. That was a relief. I was sick of being in the dark, cramped tunnels. Anything is better than this.

I crept forward, Whelan was not far behind me. I rounded the bend to see what the source of the light was. To my amazement, it was horrifying and beautiful at the same time. There were flying creatures, not unlike the Hellbugs, buzzing around and illuminating a massive cave clearing. They were almost like lightning bugs back on the surface, only a few thousand times their size. They appeared to be non-aggressive and lacked the tools to kill us, unlike the Skitters and

Hellbugs. I could see the walls dripping with some sort of slime or ooze. They were wet looking, and I honestly didn't want to brush against any of the walls in that room. Below the lightning bugs lie a terrifying sight: thousands of people were corralled together. They were just standing there. No one spoke, moved, or anything. That was more unsettling than seeing a bunch of killer monsters tearing us all apart.

I motioned for Whelan to take a look. He crept beside me to look through to the source of the light. I could tell by his reaction he was as confused, amazed, and terrified as I was.

"What the fu-" Whelan whispered, cutting himself off mid-word.

He motioned for the team to rally up. We crammed together as best as we could to speak to each other.

"There is everyone who ever lived out here down in that hole, ladies and gentlemen," Whelan started as he kept his voice as low as possible, "Local Nationals, soldiers, you name it. They're all down there. Even that dude Eriks you were hunting for," "What is it?" Dalog asked.

"Holding pens, maybe? I'm not sure, do I look like a giant freak bug expert to you, asshole?" Whelan snapped.

Dalog recoiled back.

"Geeze excuse the hell out of me for wanting to know what type of monsters we are fighting down there."

"Enough. We have to get it together and rescue these people. Maybe the lightning bugs draw them in?" I asked.

By now, everyone in the team has had the opportunity to squeeze past to see the unsettling horrors that lie beyond the cave tunnel and share in my fear.

"The fuck?" Martinez said as he crept closer to the source of the light.

X shifted a bit to the side to allow Martinez to get a better view. We must have looked like those kids from that movie Sandlot, peering over the fence at the giant dog. Unfortunately for us, we lacked the balance to stack on one another. As Martinez moved in for a better view, his foot pushed against some loose gravel. The rocks under his boot skid and crunched, tumbling down the hill after being disturbed.

The jig was up. The bugs knew we were here now if they didn't already. The lightning bugs didn't budge. They remained hovered over the crowd of bodies, undisturbed. The fact that nothing acknowledged our presence was more disturbing than being attacked at this moment. Martinez crept down the trail further. The cave opening became broader and more extensive the further into the tunnel you went. I'm not sure what compelled him to get closer, but he edged closer than I would have ever would have dreamed.

X tried to grab his attention but failed. He knelt down into a squat, resting on his haunches to stop periodically as he slowly stepped down the rocky path. Whelan shot me a look as if I should have prevented my soldier from doing something stupid. I was not known for stopping irrational behavior; instead, I encouraged it most of the time. Typically, those instances didn't involve a giant bug army. Instead, they were commenced by a lot of drinking, followed by a 'hold my beer.' This was not one of those times I'd recommend doing something ballsy. "Shit," I muttered under my breath, as I crept downward toward Martinez.

The rocks were smaller and crunchier under my boots the further I went down. I had to move a bit faster to close the distance with Martinez, who was nearing the mouth of the opening. I glanced back at the rest of the team and gestured for them to not follow. There was no need to follow where we were headed. This was a damn suicide mission. This was textbook horror movie, where the main characters check the noise in the basement. The only difference was our basement was located several clicks below the surface of the earth.

I finally made it to the side of SPC Martinez. I placed my hand on his shoulder. He jumped slightly for a moment before realizing I had crept up on him. He was so focused on what was going on, he didn't hear the high level of noise I made from my low levels of stealth.

"You see this shit, B?" Martinez asked.

I followed his gaze to what he was looking at. The Lightning Bugs weren't just providing light and a sickly ambiance, they were sprinkling some sort of powder onto the crowd below. I really didn't want to find out the hard way exactly what the dust was. The people below were very obviously from every walk of life. I could make out American civilians and soldiers alike. There were plenty of Turbans and Burkas to be seen, in addition to the rest of the traditional Iraqi garb. Judging from the color of the gear, some IA guys, the local army, fell victim to these things as well. The room was full of hundreds, if not thousands of people, all standing still.

Martinez crept a bit closer to get a better look as if getting closer would make more sense of the situation. I glanced back at the rest of the team, who were all standing around staring at the breathtaking and equally horrifying sight. Before I could readjust my gaze back to the glowing Temple of Gloom, Martinez lost his footing. The hill wasn't too steep. Couple that with a semi-steep hill with loose rocks, and that makes for a dangerously noisy cocktail. The stones and gravel ground under his boot loudly, as he slid a few feet down the hill. He came to a grinding halt, but the pebbles and debris did not. Small rocks continued to patter down the trail, cracking and popping as they hit other stones. Unlike last time we kicked rocks, this time, they heard us loud and clear.

I wish I could describe the noise that came from the Lightning Bugs as they detected us. Nothing on Earth, man-made or synthesized, is its equivalent. Imagine if you will, an elephant getting punched in the junk, while at the same time an alligator hisses through a boat fog horn. Couple all of that with Fran Drescher's voice, and that comes close. The sound was deafening. The base tone of the noise they made caused the cavern to shake and shift from the vibrations. Every human that stood under their dust was now looking up at us. If I had any food in my system, I swear I would have crapped my pants at this moment.

The bugs trumpeted once more. It was almost like a Viking battle horn signaling the start of something big. My brain knew that I had to get out of there, but my body refused to move. I was too busy staring off in amazement at what was going on. The golden power stopped falling onto the people below, and they began to move and shuffle about. I think they were preserved in a sort of stasis by that stuff. All at once, I felt a pull at the handle on the back of my vest. It was Whelan. He shot me a sharp look, and I understood clearly. We needed to the hell out of this cave.

The group of us began our climb back up the hill. The chem-lights were fading a bit but were still readily visible. Maybe they were disappearing, or perhaps they seemed fainter due to the bright room we just left. Either way, it was just enough to know the way. Whelan pushed his way to the front of the pack with Jacobson just to his left. Martinez brought up the rear of the group with X. I stayed in the middle with Dalog, Mr. Jarrett and Rogers. We all subconsciously knew something big was about to go down. It was either the most significant fight we'd ever seen, or this cave was going to come crashing down on us. Either way, we didn't want any parts of it.

Debris fell from the ceiling of the cavern tunnel as we ran. Pieces of cave landed on my helmet and made me glad I wore the thing. We could see the transition in colors of the chem-lights where X ran out of yellow and switched to blue. We were getting closer to the fork in the tunnel. We came to the mouth of the cavern path we took, and something told me to look to my left down the road not yet traveled. I shifted my head to peek into the dark cave trail as we passed it.

I heard screeching and other unsettling noises. Something was coming through the cave behind us. We needed to get out in the open and face these things head-on.

"Just up ahead! C'mon!" Whelan bellowed, gesturing toward the daylight cave mouth ahead.

# Chapter 14

*Yawm Jayid, IZ*
*1630 Local*
*February 13, 2010*

I could tell it was getting darker outside, but the light was still blinding. It was near sunset at this point. Terrified, I decided to what is advised against in every horror movie: I looked back. Just a few meters behind Martinez, I could see a swarm of shadow covered Skitter Critters. My heart sank into my boots, making it harder to run. Martinez knew better than to look behind him. We were almost at the cave opening now, and gunfire would be warranted.

As the first of us thrust through the entrance of the cavern, a Hellbug swooped by. Before any of us could react or retreat, a second one swooped down. The screech the beast made panged through our ears. Its claws outstretched, it gripped onto Jacobson. Whelan pushed forward and aimed his weapon and took several accurate shots at the Hellbug. I emerged from the cave just in time to see his shots land perfectly into the wings of the creature. It let out a roar-like screech before slowly falling to the ground. I let out a small sigh of relief thanks to Whelan's accuracy.

The relief was short-lived as the second Hellbug came in and collected Jacobson from the falling Hellbug. The injured one tried desperately to hang on to its airborne status. The two gripped

Jacobson as he screamed and tried to fight off the creatures. Whelan took aim once more as the two Hellbugs ascended higher into the atmosphere. They were so far, I'm positive with good luck on my side I'd never make that shot. Even if I did, chances are the fall would kill Jacobson.

Gunshots cracked across the open desert air as Whelan fired three consecutive shots, each a few seconds apart. He took aim for a fourth shot. This one hit. Just as the bugs were high enough and damn near unrecognizable to me, Whelan hit. Jacobson's body went limp as the two bugs carted him off to some unknown fate.

"It's what I'd want you to do for me, kid," Whelan said as he moved away from the cave mouth.

He just landed a several hundred yards or more iron sited mercy killing. I'm disgusted and impressed.

"Here they come!" Dalog shouted, readying his rifle as he backed away from the cave mouth.

We each readied our weapons in anticipation of the horde about to emerge from the mineshaft cavern entrance. Each of us was walking backward, putting distance between us and the cave each step we took. One by one, Skitter Critters crawled out of the mouth of the cave. Immediately we opened fire on them before they could adjust to the fading daylight. With each carcass, a barricade was formed at the entrance. The next Skitter struggled to break through the pile of its comrades' bodies, only to become part of the blockage.

"Like shooting fish in a barrel!" Rogers yelled.

"Don't get cocky," Whelan snapped.

Martinez moved to the side to get a better view of the opening. The mouth of the cave was well stuffed with bodies at this point. I saw his expression shift from satisfied to concerned. I left our kill squad to continue to pump bullets into the small opening in the cave entrance, following Martinez to what he was looking at.

On top of the entrance, the sand was being disturbed. I could make out the faintest bit of a claw that began to protrude from the dirt as it scraped and clawed. The beasts were making a new exit.

"Shit! Fall back! Fall back!" I screamed to the rest of the group.

No sooner than screaming out that command, Whelan noticed precisely what I was screaming about. A Skitter had emerged waist-high out of the sand, presumably using it's fallen brethren as a step stool. One by one, they pierced through the sandy walls that surrounded the entrance.

"Right. Let's get the hell out of here. Y'all make it to the entrance of the base and don't stop," Whelan commanded.

I didn't ask questions. I didn't debate. I ran. Alexopoulos ran. Martinez was ahead of all of us with his feet double-timing it. None of us wasted time. I glanced around while running to see that everyone who was in our squad was hauling as much ass as I was. Even Mr. Jarrett was running hard enough to be qualified for Army physical fitness standards.

Sand dune by sand dune, we ran. Our boots were slipping and sliding in the loose grains, but that didn't stop us. I could see the base up ahead in the distance. By my guess, it was a few kilometers away. I was hopeful that we would make it to the base with enough space between us and the creatures to get a bit of a resupply as well. I decided to break the horror movie rules and looked behind us. I felt the heat on my neck as I knew Dalog was glaring at me for breaking one of the golden rules.

"I think we're safe. They're not behind us anymore," I said as ironically as possible knowing Dalog was judging me.

The group came to a halt from running. The sound of catching breath filled the air as everyone gasped for oxygen. I continued to look around, wiping the sweat from my face. It was all clear. We survived the cave of death.

"Sweet! How about next adventure, we go see if we can fight a dragon?

Maybe a giant troll that is guarding some gold? I call Bard this time!" Dalog said sarcastically.

"Somethin' wrong with ya? Ya got a screw or some'n lose?" Rogers asked angrily.

Dalog's smile wiped away from his face. I get it. It's his way of coping. We all have our own ways of dealing with trauma, and comedy isn't unheard of. Some guys shut down. Some guys get angry. This guy apparently wraps his brain around the situation by believing he's in some first-person shooter video game. Whatever gets him through the day and keeps him grounded. Well, as grounded as one could be with believing he's the Legend of Zelda or something. I could tell the video game schtick was getting on Whelan's crew's nerves.

"Listen up. I don't know what the hell we are doing, but you guys need to get your heads out of your fifth points of contact, yeah?" Whelan began, "so while you kids are out here smokin' and jokin', the grownups are trying to survive."

His gaze fell directly on Dalog. I don't think Whelan understood precisely what we have been through to know that we want to live and want to keep pushing through this shitshow.

"You damn Pogues are more fucked up than a box full of football bats, and it shows. You've never seen combat a day in your insignificant little lives, have you?" Whelan belted out as he kicked some sand around with his boot.

I had a feeling that he had been a Drill Instructor of some sorts while he was in the service. Whelan was noticeably older than the rest of our lot, save for Mr. Jarrett. I was getting hardcore Marine or combat-based vibes from him since we met. His motivational speech almost solidified that.

"So, what's the plan now, B?" Martinez said, taking his helmet to wipe some sweat off of his shaved head.

"First off, I'm not your B. Second off, I don't have the slightest fucking clue, Hos. I'm flying blind, balls first into a minefield. But I had an idea back at the city," Whelan grunted.

"Care to share that plan with the rest of the class?" X asked, asserting herself to Whelan.

"Woah now, missy. Don't get your panties twisted," Rogers laughed, putting his hand on her shoulder.

X quickly grabbed his hand and twisted it in about twenty different ways. I've never seen such a large man belt out a whelp like that before. I shot X a look, and after a few more seconds, she let him go. Rogers nursed his forearm for a few minutes before clearing his throat to speak up.

"So, there's this idea we been talkin' 'bout. They got the planes and stuff on base, and we needs to be there. I got some flight hours, flown a plane or two in my day. We gotta get to another base," Rogers said, flexing his arm to work out the pain.

I stood up immediately.

"The base is a no go, my man," I quickly asserted.

Mr. Jarrett nodded in agreement.

Whelan didn't seem amused by my answer.

"Word. That base is pretty messed up. We already got out of there once, I'm not trying to go back," Mr. Jarrett said.

I'm not sure if the words coming from us were insignificant, or if they sounded better coming from a guy in an Eagles jersey, but Rogers whole expression changed. Whelan seemed to be listening more intently.

"Ok. We can't go barging into the base like we own the place. It's getting darker out, we gotta play it safe. Y'all been on that base how long?" Whelan asked.

"Six months," I said.

"Too damn long," Martinez added.

"Hmm," Whelan brushed his red beard with his hand, "What's the path that would keep us off the main road, but get us to that flight line?"

I thought long and hard for a bit. First and foremost, I thought about where the hell we were going to go once we were airborne. Was this isolated? Is this global? Maybe Dalog is onto something, and this is apocalyptic. What if home is destroyed? The more I thought about everything, the more I felt depressed.

"I've been on this base for damn near a year and a half. I got you," Mr. Jarrett said to Whelan.

"Oh, well at least someone around here is useful. What's the best way to sneak around off the main roads?"

"I'm thinking the way we ran through trying to get out of that crazy mess," Mr. Jarrett responded.

Whelan shifted his expression and lowered his shoulders.

"Care to fill me in on that egress route?" Whelan said, after letting out a defeated sigh.

Mr. Jarrett had a solid idea. This was actually the most he's really contributed to Operation Don't Die since we started trying to not die a few days ago. I figured he was holding on to more abilities than he let on. He and Whelan discussed a plan to get through the base privately. I was curious why the two didn't share with us. After all, we had been saving asses this whole time from where I stood.

"Ok, here's the plan," Whelan announced as he turned to face the team, "We're going in the east checkpoint gate. It's got a lot of overhead cover. That should help for a few moments to keep Hellbugs off our ass."

He stopped to look around for a moment as if saying the very name would summon one to fight.

"Once we are through, we will head to the Air Force compound. It's walled, and harder to sneak up on us. After that, we beeline it, two by two to the airstrip. Copy?" Whelan commanded.

"Copy," everyone echoed.

Whelan started to walk toward the base as he cracked his back and neck. With each step, he bent his legs as if stretching as he moved. Probably not a bad idea to limber up, given what we've seen so far. The group began to stand and follow him through the sands toward the base.

"Once at the airfield, Rogers here will start up the first functional piece of aircraft he can get his little dickbeaters onto. Damn any supplies, we will fly to wherever we can find that's closest and not on fire," Whelan's voice drifted off as he ventured further from my position.

It sounded like a solid plan. Get to the base, get to a plane, get gone. I dig it, and it's no better than I could come up with. At least we had a pilot that could get us safely to the air. I'd have likely buried the plane in the sand six feet from the takeoff location. But we were doing it. I double-timed it and tried to catch up with X and Martinez, who were engaged in conversation.

"I just need to see anything normal at this point, for real," Martinez said.

"Yeah. Food and a shower would be a nice touch," replied X.

I finally managed to match pace with them and chimed in.

"I just need to get off this butthole of a base, city, and country," I said.

Everyone smiled and nodded. Dalog must have heard because he chuckled a bit after my comment. I picked up the pace a bit and caught up to Whelan and Rogers. They were up front and pushing forward harder than ever. I almost struggled to keep pace.

"So, this plan, will it work?" I asked, realizing how stupid I must have sounded.

"*Of course* it will work. Mr. Jarrett said he knows some of the ways in and out of the base. Couple that with kicking ass, taking names and my good looks, and we're gold," Whelan laughed.

I smiled a bit, not sure how to respond at all. I was sure glad to find these guys when we did because we didn't have a clue what we were doing.

"So, what did you used to do, you know, before this?" I asked.

Whelan looked over at me. His expression softened a bit. I felt like he was about to open up to me.

"Eleven-Bang Bang. Did ten years in the Army. Had a hell of a run too. Five or six tours under my belt. Lost count after the fourth. Fallujah, Baghdad, and some other places I couldn't tell you the names of. Not that I can't, I just couldn't pronounce the fuckers. Give me an easy name, like Dallas, Arlington, hell, even Midland. Easy shit. America is good for that, at least," Whelan said, smiling a bit as he talked about Texas.

"You're a Texas guy, right?" I asked, again, feeling stupid after my obvious answers were in front of me.

He smiled at me, raising an eyebrow.

"You ask a lot of dumb shit when you're terrified, don't you?" he asked.

"Nah, I usually ask dumb shit all the time. This is just me."

"Yeah, I'm a Texan, born and bred. Once this shit started to hit the fan, I immediately wanted to get back to Plano by any means necessary," said Whelan.

"Plano? Where is that at?" I asked.

"Plano? Oh, it's up north Texas. Famous little spot, ya know? They filmed that show Dallas just south there. Probably don't even know that show, kid," Whelan said dismissively.

I thought about it for a moment. I knew that show and heard enough about it to understand what Whelan meant. I never actually watched Dallas.

"What about you, kid. You got any place you'd rather be?"

"Virginia. That's home. I lived south of DC. Spitting distance to there and Baltimore."

"Baltimore? That shithole? Speaking of TV shows, how about The Wire? They filmed that there, I think. Can't think of nothin' out there in Virginia. Maybe them X-Files?" Whelan said, showing visible contemplation of famous television shows.

I shrugged my shoulders a bit. I honestly wasn't sure what shows filmed in my town, but X-Files seemed reasonable enough.

"Hell, I sound like your Asian friend back there, talking about TV Shows and X-Files and shit," Whelan laughed as he shot a glance over to Dalog.

"Family?" I asked, hoping to not be overstepping boundaries.

"One ex-wife, two daughters, and a fiancée," Whelan said.

I didn't want to chime in on the ex-wife, or why she was even mentioned as family. I assumed they must be on good terms, or the kid's mom or something. Not my place to question.

"What about you, Chantry? Got family back in the States?" Whelan prodded.

"Not really. I have a few aunts, uncles, cousins. Both my parents passed already. No lady waiting for me back home either," I said.

I hadn't really thought about what I don't have to go home to, until now. I had no one. No parents worried sick about the news stories coming from Iraq. No girlfriend or wife to get back to. Nothing.

"Damn, kid. That's rough. But you're young, you'll find a lady one day. Just don't pick the wrong one."

The three of us kept pace up at the front for the rest of the walk. Our in-depth talk took my mind off of the heat and setting sun as we stomped through the desert. It was nice to actually have a human conversation. It was even more helpful to have a conversation with the guy who wouldn't give me two words when we first met.

"Marine. If you were asking," Rogers added, "No family. I got a dog, though. Habanero is his name. Small little wiener dog that I thought looked like a pepper. It wasn't until I put his name on the paperwork at the vet that I realized habanero peppers aren't long like the dog. But it stuck. I'm cool with it."

I chuckled. It's about time these guys were opening up. I could tell the rest of the group was listening in on the conversation as well.

We did our best to exchange small talk and stories of our hometowns, school, military time, and more. That filled in the void and killed time. I barely noticed how far we walked as the walls of the base came into view. The base didn't look too worse for wear. Heck, you wouldn't even know shit hit the fan from the outside.

"Still standing, I see. Ole' Centurion. I missed the old girl," Rogers said.

"I'd like to keep missing it if at all possible," Dalog added.

We continued our course and closed the distance on the checkpoint entrance. It was empty, abandoned, and entirely disheveled. Story of our lives.

"From here, we need to follow Jarrett down his shortcut. Get to the planes and take the hell off. Got it?" Whelan commanded.

"Copasetic," replied Dalog.

The rest of us nodded in agreement. If we were getting off this godforsaken base and far from this nightmare, this was our best chance.

We had to fly.

# Chapter 15

*FOB Centurion, IZ*
*2245 Local*
*February 13, 2010*

It was late. The sun had set. The moon provided us with much-needed illumination in the blackened environment. The lack of people made the setting much more terrifying. There was a calming stillness to the air, however. It was almost like the late-night walks I'd take to ease my mind. The only difference was that there was no mind easing taking place tonight. Survival was on the brain, and getting out was the ticket.

I knew following Whelan and Rogers was probably the best choice I've made this whole ordeal. I didn't have the slightest idea of how to lead at all. It's just a relief to know I don't have the pressures of figuring out things. Whelan had it all figured out. Get the first flight out of this dump and throw a match on the gasoline on the way out. My plan involved curling in a ball, soiling myself, all while seeking out the next idea. Figures it would only make sense I'd latch on to the first authoritative figure that came by.

"The checkpoint is clear. There's nobody out here. Nothing, and nobody. That's not cool. I don't like this, Holmes," Martinez said as he kicked over an empty box.

I agreed with a slight nod. I could tell Whelan and X agreed as well with the change in their expression. Something about a completely dead base was troublesome. We knew where everyone was though; inside a cave buried deep underground. I still had questions about that whole situation, let alone whatever the hell the rest of these things that were trying to kill us were. I wasn't in a position to understand anything whatsoever.

"Bruh. The final stage, man," Dalog said as he checked his rifle for a chambered round.

I heard Whelan let out an audible sigh. I can't blame him, Dalog has been adamant that this whole thing has been a video game or a movie since the start of it. Part of me was growing annoyed with it too. I followed Whelan forward as we crept slowly through the checkpoint. Slowly creeping along the tall barricaded wall, we kept an ear out for anything that sounded like it could kill us.

Whelan stopped at the end of the barrier of the checkpoint. He motioned to Mr. Jarrett to move up to where he was at.

"Ok, so we need to get through here. That's obvious. You said you know the safest route to stay off the radar of these fuckers?" asked Whelan.

"Word. I got this, stay close," Mr. Jarrett said confidently.

We all nodded and carried on, following closely behind Mr. Jarrett. I gripped my rifle a little harder after crossing into the base. The thoughts of what we endured not a day or so ago passed across my thoughts all at once. The people we lost, along with the carnage we witnessed. How did we even make it this far? The thoughts kept my brain busy as we crept behind tight spaces tucked behind buildings.

We squeezed through the Air Force area with ease. I could feel that all of us had the same thought going through our heads. I knew we were all asking ourselves where the hell the Critters were. If we weren't asking that, we sure as shit should have been. We were about due for another attack.

"Shits quiet. Too quiet," Martinez said as he looked through the window of an operations building.

"Fuck. Off. You don't say shit like that in a horror movie, man. You trying to get us killed out here?" Dalog scoffed.

Whelan finally had enough of the nerd chatter from Dalog. He whirled around and grabbed him by his top and pressed him hard against the barricade.

"Jesus Fucking Christ. If you don't drop this bullshit right now, I'll pull you right out of the fucking Matrix right now. You'll log off for good, hear?" Whelan barked.

Dalog nodded in agreement. He adjusted his glasses as Whelan loosened his grip. I figured that was bound to happen. But Dalog was right, sort of. You don't say that kind of stuff in situations like this, movie or otherwise.

We continued to follow Mr. Jarrett through several winding turns and twists in between the barriers and buildings in the Air Force complex. I'd never been over to this side of the base before, so this was all new to me. We approached a large utility station at a clearing. It looked like a sewage treatment or something as far as I could tell, but it lacked the horrendous smell of one. There was something that looked like a pump on top. Maybe it was a water well.

"Ok, this is it. You guys lift up this grate here. Once we in, we go through some tunnels. On the other side, we will pop out of the other side of the base. From there, we backtrack a bit to the airfield. Best I can do," Mr. Jarret explained.

Martinez pushed past everyone and gripped one of the handles of the grate. I decided to grab another. It was heavier than I thought it would be, but I pretended to have control of the situation. It took everything in my body to not yell obscenities and complain about the weight. After sliding the cover enough to fit bodies inside, I dropped the handle. That was going to be the death of my back if I moved it again.

I turned on of the flashlights on and shined the light inside the tunnel.

It seemed quiet and regular enough for me.

"I'll go first," X said as she lowered herself into the tunnel shaft entrance.

I didn't really have much say in stopping her from being the first to dive into the most dangerous idea we'd come across. Actually, so far, we had done some pretty stupid things since this whole thing started. This was right in the fray of crazy. If I had to rate it, however, I'd toss this on a solid ten on a scale of one to crazy.

"Chantry, you're up," Whelan said, gesturing toward the open manhole entrance.

"Gee, I'm honored. Thanks, buddy," I snapped back sarcastically.

I lowered myself into the hole. Surprisingly it wasn't as tight a fit as I initially thought. I half expected to get snagged halfway in, getting fully Winnie The Pooh'd and wait around to die from a Skitter or something. But I slid right through with room to spare. Even with all of this gear on, it worked out.

I touched down on the ground after about a foot or two worth of freefalling. It wasn't enough to get hurt, but enough to sure as hell give you a bit of a pucker factor. It was pretty dark in the tunnel. I could barely make out the figure of X in the distance. If not for her flashlight, I'd have no idea where the hell she was at. I didn't like this one bit. I heard another person lowering into the shaft. I couldn't tell you who it was because of the darkness.

"Oh, great! A sewer stage," Dalog said, identifying who the unknown body was dropping in beside me.

An audible sigh came from the top side of the grate entrance. I could tell Whelan was one more video game or movie reference away from burying a fist into Dalog's skull. His body landed with a loud crash into the small amount of water than lay stagnant on the ground.

"Oh, Christ it smells down here," Whelan said as he covered his face.

I hadn't honestly noticed the smell. Now that it was brought up,

I could pick up the mildew and mold overtones that floated down through the tunnel. I really hoped this was worth it. I didn't want to get sick for nothing. Bad enough the burn pits probably blackened my lungs like a steak left too long on a grill. I didn't need any help from this tunnel to make it worse.

Once everyone had lowered into the tunnel, I flattened to the side to allow Mr. Jarrett to pass to the front of the pack. X stuck by his side, followed closely by Whelan. I think he wanted to know how this was going to play out as much as I did. We began to creep through the tunnel system. It was concrete-walled, lined with various electrical and communication lines throughout. This must have been some sort of utility tunnel to make it easier to run power through the base.

"It's about ten minutes or so. Plus, I gotta stop for a smoke," Mr. Jarrett said as he pushed some low hanging wires out of his way.

Whelan shot a look at the back of the group. We made eye contact, so I assumed he was giving me a look to question what we were doing. It wasn't until I realized he was looking through me, that I noticed his gaze was set to his partner Rogers. That's always awkward. It's like seeing someone wave to you, and you wave back like an idiot, only to realize you have no idea who that person is. It was mainly that feeling creeping through my spine as I broke eye contact.

Rogers nodded back to him as if there was some underlying 'bro signals' going on that I didn't know. I needed to know what was going on. I let Dalog and Martinez push past me in the tunnel. I dropped back far enough to match pace with Rogers.

"What the hell is going on with you guys?" I whispered.

Whelan wiped the side of his nose with the back of his hand. It looked like he was visibly trying to dodge my question.

"Well?"

"Don't trust 'im," Rogers said under his breath.

"Clearly. Mr. Jarrett's been working with our unit for a while, he's good people. I never really knew what he did, though. I vouch for him being a good dude, though. So, what's your beef with him?" I questioned.

Rogers sighed. He adjusted his three-point sling to lower his rifle a bit.

"It's just, he's been pretty useless since ya got whacked by us up on that roof. He ain't really shootin' nuthin'. All of a sudden, Mr. Hotshot has a secret tunnel to get us to safety? That don't seem a bit crazy to you?"

I thought about that for a second. It really was awfully convenient that this tunnel situation popped up. Why wasn't this used as we tried to leave this place? It's also unusually safe down here. We could have used this and maybe preserved a few lives. Eriks, Captain Seeker, Sergeant Matthews. Any one of these guys could still be with us if we jumped in this tunnel to start.

"You're startin' to doubt this whole thing too, ain'tcha?" Rogers asked.

I nodded slightly. As I drifted off into my brain to digest everything that was going on, I decided to close the gap on the rest of the pack. I shifted up the tunnel around everyone, catching pace with Dalog.

"Still think this is a game, dude?" I asked, jabbing my elbow into the side of his body armor.

He let out a little laugh.

"Man, if I let you all in on half of the things that were bouncing around in my brain, you'd think I was crazy," Dalog chuckled as he said.

I shook my head and laughed back at him.

"It's gonna be fine. Jarrett is taking is through the base. These guys can fly shit. They want to get out of the shitshow and back home as much as we do," I said, trying to do my best to reassure him.

I may have been trying to reassure myself. I'm not really sure at this point.

"Sweet. I'm just worried you know?"

"About?"

"What's on the other end of that tunnel? Do we even know?"
"Bug monster from Venus, bro!" Martinez chimed in.

I didn't really know what to respond with. I smiled. At least the thought of something preposterous on the other end was more reassuring than whatever was ready to eat us alive.
"Almost there," Mr. Jarrett said to the group.

I noticed the group quickened the pace a bit. The thought of getting out of this intestine of the base was a solid priority. I have to admit, I moved with a fire lit myself.
"Here!" Mr. Jarrett said as he stopped.

He pointed upward as at a sealed door. It had a large handle coated in cobwebs. I really hoped we didn't have to deal with mutant Camel Spiders. I could do without that being added to the mix. Mr. Jarrett sat against the piping that led through a concrete wall that ended the tunnel. He pulled a Black and Mild cigar from his back pocket. I was shocked that it was still intact after everything we've been through.
"What the fuck are you doing?" Whelan barked.

Mr. Jarrett shifted against the pipe, checking through his pockets.

"What? I was clear with what I was going to do. Get to the end of the tunnel, spark a Black."

"We need to get the fuck off this shithole! Why do you think we can fit this into our busy schedule?" Whelan snapped.

Mr. Jarrett slid the cigar back into his front pocket.

"Lucky I can't find my lighter. After you, my man," Jarrett said, gesturing to the hatch.

Whelan reached up and gripped the handle with both hands and pulled. It moaned with a rusty squeak.

"Stuck," Whelan grunted as he pulled the door handle.

Dalog reached forward and put a hand on the open part of the handle latch. Together, the two of them moved it further. Dalog and Whelan both lowered their arms.

"Jesus that's in there," Whelan expressed as he shook out his arms.

"Let's hit it again, brother," Whelan said to Dalog.

Both reached up once more, this time putting a foot against the sidewall to give more leverage. Martinez stepped forward and threw his weight into the remaining few inches of the handle that was left exposed. It squealed loudly as it gave way.

"Come through here often, eh?" Whelan looked toward Mr. Jarrett.

"Word. I never said I came through here, I said I knew about it."

Whelan looked visibly upset but managed to brush it off and pushed the door open. The night sky was visible as ever. I hadn't looked up at it for a while, given all of the chaos. I forgot how nice it actually looked. Clearly, with this invasion of creatures we are having, it really makes sense to not be alone in the universe out there.

"Chantry!" Rogers yelled.

I must have daydreamed up at the night sky and lost myself. The team had pushed through the doorway already. It was just Rogers and me. I shook it off and gripped the small ladder that lead upward. As I hoisted myself to the surface, I felt uneasy. I wasn't sure what was wrong, but there was a feeling. It's like that thing Spider-Man has, my sense was tingling. I immediately scrambled to my feet. We were practically back where we started. This tunnel was just a few minute's walk from headquarters. How did I never know about this?

I reached back and assisted Rogers through the entrance.

"Thanks, brother," he muttered.

We huddled around in the clearing.

"Ok, we know where we are. It's a click and change to get over to the airfield," Whelan said.

Martinez nodded. I was in and out through the conversation. I kept feeling like something was off. I heard something shift in the night sky. Something was off.

"Shit! There!" Whelan yelled, pointing his rifle just past my head.

I turned around and saw what he meant. Four Skitters coming our direction. I've handled much worse. A few gunshots rattled off near my head. X and Martinez had already begun laying fire at them. We just rang the dinner bell again.

I heard movement to my right. Just over the barricades, I saw a Big and Nasty grunting its way toward the action. Its arms raised and begun glowing blue. The gunfire increased. My head whirled around, looking at the surroundings. More Skitters had joined the pack thanks to the noise we were making. It was game over.

I shouldered my rifle. I began taking careful shots at the Skitters. We never discovered a weak spot or the right place to shoot. I figured the face was a hell of a start. I saw their oily crazy blood spraying out of their bodies. One by one, they began to collapse. Thank god that our regular bullets worked. I couldn't imagine needing special ammo.

I squeezed off another two or three rounds before I realized I forgot about the Big and Nasty.

"Big and Nasty, Three O'clock!" I screamed over the gunfire.

No sooner than I yelled, did a sizeable blue bolt of energy ball crackle overhead. It just missed us by about a foot. I turned my focus toward the big bastard. It was too far to do any real damage to it. I needed to get close.

"Moving on the B and N!" I belted out as I fired a few rounds at the now increasingly massive horde of Skitters.

I figured the lot of us could handle Skitter Critters. These things were predictable to a degree. Hell, everything we've come across has had some sort of pattern of predictability. I moved around the other side of the barrier wall that separated the Big and Nasty from the team. I trained the barrel of my rifle on its right cannon arm.

Squeezing the trigger gently, I fired off shot after shot. Each connected with a visible blood spatter.

I ran from cover to cover as I fired off an entire magazine of rounds into the fist. The audible click of that ever-dreaded 'out of ammo' sound hit. I dropped the magazine and slammed a fresh one into the weapon and slapped the bolt forward. I continued my barrage of trained rounds into the arm. I started to notice something; the arm was being severed by my bullets.

I had apparently launched enough into a concentrated area that it began to cut through the meat. That motivated me to keep going. I moved closer as I fired. The Big and Nasty let out a pain-filled roar as I saw the right fist peel away from the rest of its arm. I felt satisfied, wishing someone was nearby to hear a pun about disarming it.

It was hurt, but not dead. It had charged up the left fist in the haze of my celebration. A blue ball of lightning emerged from its fist. From the side, it seemed even more comically slow. How was this supposed to be a significant threat? I began to fire rounds into its face much as I had before. The Big and Nasty coiled back in pain. I changed magazines once more. Damn, last mag. I had to make this count.

I squeezed rounds off faster than before. A squeal that sounded like a group of dying pigs came from the creature. The Big and Nasty went limp. It didn't entirely fall over. Instead, it slumped in position. Close enough for me. I cheered to myself, pumping my fist in celebration. I looked over to see what else we had left to deal with. I couldn't move fast enough. I couldn't yell. I just stood on the mound of rocks and dead Big and Nasty in horror.

The blue ball of light had drifted toward the crew. I don't know if

Martinez saw it before I did, or if we caught it at the same time. There was nothing that could be done. I looked into his eyes as the energy engulfed his body. His clothing, body armor, weapon; everything was absorbed. There was an audible sizzle as his body burned a bright blue before what remained of his body collapsed in a heap.

My feet were more onerous than ever. I dragged myself back to the group. I don't know if everyone had noticed what happened. As I rounded the corner of the barrier, I realized the gunfire stopped. The now quiet air was filled with shouts of denial and remorse.

"Fucking shit! Fucking shit!" X yelled out as she knelt over Martinez.

I moved toward his body. What remained was glowing blue. Part of his head, an arm and some of his torso and a leg was all that lay behind of Specialist Diego Martinez. He didn't deserve this. He was a leader, a fighter, and an all-around badass. It should have been me. I should have fired harder and disabled both arms. I dropped back against the short barricade wall behind me, sliding to the ground.

Whelan, as tough a guy as he was, even took a moment. He punched one of the carcasses of a Skitter pretty hard, breaking a part of it off as he did.

"We– We have to keep going," Rogers muttered.

X was visibly crying over his body. Dalog wandered away from the area, obviously trying to process what just happened.

"I think. I think we should take five, Whelan," I said, standing to my feet.

I did all I could to hold back my emotions. I didn't have the luxury of a pitch-black arms room like before. The last breakdown I had was surrounded by bullets in a locked room.

"We. Have. To. Move," Whelan sounded out.

Goddamnit. As much as I wanted to hit him for his insensitivity, I ultimately got it. We had to get moving.

"Can we have a fucking second!" X yelled while holding back a guttural cry.

It was unanimous, we needed a second. We'd seen people carried away, possessed, and eviscerated. I don't think we were mentally prepared to see someone vaporized and disintegrated.

"Fine. Ten minutes and we move out. It's not like we are missing a flight time," Whelan said.

I took the time we were so graciously given to mourn and get off my feet. I realized Dalog had wandered off and didn't return yet. I stifled my tears and emotions a bit and stood back up. I couldn't lose another guy.

# Chapter 16

*FOB Centurion, IZ*
*0015 Local*
*February 14, 2010*

I must have wandered through and between a dozen buildings. It was the dumbest thing I had ever done, and that's saying a lot.

What part of my brain switched on and decided 'hey, we're going to walk through this monster-infested warzone alone' anyhow? I walked back over to the headquarters building. I'm not sure what forced my legs to trod over that direction, but we were going there regardless. I was on autopilot. I had physically, mentally, and emotionally shut down. Maybe it was an instinct that drove me back to work?

I turned the corner that opened up to the street way that housed our headquarters building. It was dark and smelled awful. The smell of death filled the air full of a putrid stank. That's a smell you never forget, death. Particularly when speaking about old death. I could only assume the body of Studds or Sergeant Matthews was sitting around half-eaten, slowly rotting away somewhere in the most disrespectful fashion. They deserved better. Especially Studds, since he had a kid on the way.

I recovered from my haze of daydreaming to realize I had entered the headquarters building. I slowly moved down the ramp that lowered me into the main hallway. The radio was silent. The building was darker than I had ever seen it. Fumbling for my flashlight, I pressed my thumb on the switch, blasting a beam of bright LED light into the room. It was eerie, and I could barely contain my emotions as I looked at what was now an alien world to me.

I passed by the radio desk. I glanced down, spotting a half-read copy of 'Ranch Hand Seduction" laying on the radio. I'll admit, I choked up just a bit. I reached down slowly and grabbed the book, opening it to the page he was on last. He was about halfway through the book, it seemed. His bookmark was a photo of his girlfriend from back in New York, I think. I never met the girl, but it was safe to assume he knew her. I pulled it out of the book to give it a better look with the flashlight. She was pretty. I flipped the photo over.

On the reverse side of the photo, there was a note. 'Come back to me in one piece, D. Love, Francesca.' Christ. My heart was so heavy it may as well have landed across the Earth through the core. I was so caught up in the book, photo, and memories that I didn't even notice the grip something had on my shoulder. I felt the pressure squeeze. My blood ran cold, and I froze up. I figured whatever had me was going to make it quick.

"Calm the fuck down, dude. It's me," Dalog said, removing his hand from my shoulder.

I placed the book back down on the radio. I hesitated for a second, then picked it back up and jammed it into my bag. I figured we might want to honor Martinez' memory somehow.

"It's literally the loudest door on the planet. Sorry if I scared you," Dalog continued.

I shrugged. I was still at a loss for words.

"Man, I don't know how the hell you guys worked in this place. It's so stiff and boring feeling," Dalog joked as he pushed some stacks of reports to the floor.

I sat down in Martinez' chair. I let the air out of my lungs audibly, showing that I was not in a good place.

"You good, dude?" Dalog asked as he dragged a chair across the room from my old office.

I put my hands on my face and leaned back in the chair.

"No," I started, "I'm not okay, for the record. I'm pretty fucked up.

How you doing?"

"Well, I'd imagine this is the part where we have the heart to heart bromance scene. We will rally ourselves in prep for the giant boss fight that's just outside the door."

I sat up. I don't know if I was angry or disappointed. I may have been both. Dalog's been making jokes and turning this whole disaster into a goddamn game to him. I was done. I stood up and hovered inches from his face.

"Listen. I don't know what the hell you're getting out of downplaying this and making it a goddamn game, but people are fucking dying man! Why don't you see that? It's not a video game. We aren't in Doom or Call of any kind of Duty or whatever the fuck you guys play these days. We aren't questing in a dungeon. We are surviving and being slaughtered while doing so," I went off for so long, and so hard I had to take a deep breath to recover.

"Ok. So, what you're saying is that you're not cool with all of this?" Dalog added.

My expression shifted. I didn't have it in me to argue or deal with this.

"Yes, I'm not cool with this. Are you?"

"No. I'm actually not at all ok with anything that's going on. I've been telling myself it's a video game just to get through this and not eat a fucking bullet and be done. It's literally the only thing that's been keeping me standing. Sorry if it's bothering the hell out of you."

I sat back down in the chair. I hadn't thought about this. It's a coping mechanism. The Army always told us in the training briefings and death by slideshow meetings that people have different ways to cope. Some shut down, while others open up. There are some people who get angry, and others that make jokes. Maybe Dalog was on the joke side? I never really considered how much this was messing with him. I only saw the surface.

"Jesus, dude. I didn't know," I started, "sorry for snapping." Dalog relaxed a bit in the chair.

"I don't know what would have happened if you guys didn't barge into the gym. I literally watched Sergeant Aloho, and Private Daly get decimated right in front of me. I ran. I ran far away," "Couldn't get away?" I chimed in.

He smiled. I think he appreciated my bad eighty's reference.

"Yeah, basically. I locked into that gym and just started to consider how I was getting out of all this, right? I didn't have a gun or anything, so fuck me, right?"

"Well, we're going to make it. Whelan and them are going to fire up something on the airstrip, and we are flying from this hell hole. The first contact we make with people, we're sending them back with the biggest firebomb America can make," I reassured.

He smiled a bit at the idea of this place being leveled. I'm not sure if it was the monsters or just the idea of this place we've been stuck at for the past several months being vaporized. I wasn't going to question him.

"What's the plan, dude? Go back to the crew and bounce?" Dalog asked.

I nodded. I panned around the room once more to see if anything of importance was left behind. Then it hit me. It was as if several days ago replayed in my head. I saw Studds get grabbed. I saw SGT Matthews get taken down in the street outside. I remembered why; the arms room key.

"Fuck! Bro, the arms room is open!" I exclaimed as I started for the door, "come on!"

I never moved faster in my life. I forgot we were right here, with the door being unlocked. We were about to shoot our way off this rock once more. I grabbed the door handle and ripped it open. The squeal of the door whistled through the quiet night air. I didn't care. I kept moving. My weapon was at the ready, finger ready to fire. I kept on a swivel as I walked across the wide street. Dalog wasn't too far behind. The door was slightly ajar. I kicked it open with my foot and shined the flashlight into the room. Nothing. Thank god.

"Empty. Let's do this," I called back to Dalog.

The two of us were like children that were let loose in a Toys R Us with a triple-digit value gift card. We didn't know whether to cry, smile, scream, or all three at once. As he stepped into the doorway, Dalog saw walls lined with shelves full of ammunition. Box upon box filled the room with every round you could dream of. It was a satisfying feeling remembering such a great find.

"Gearing up for the boss fight now."

I shook my head at his comment as he loaded pouches and compartments of his bag with 5.56 rounds. We were cracking open cardboard cases like they were eggs for breakfast. We couldn't break them down fast enough. There was barely any dialogue exchanged between the two of us, save for the occasional 'ooh' or 'oh man!' I couldn't wait to get back to the group. We really needed a win today. We've lost so many people, seen so much shit. I just couldn't deal with it anymore. I

was probably at my breaking point ages ago, it just hadn't sunk in yet.

"How the hell is the Army going to explain this shit to us, though?" Dalog said as he ripped open another cardboard container.

"Explain what?"

"The bugs."

*Oh. Right. Those bugs.*

"I'm just curious how they're going to spin this. It sure as hell ain't swamp gas, hot air balloons or nothing. I'd accept Bigfoot and the Loch Ness Monster as an explanation at this point."

I rubbed the back of my neck. I hadn't really given much thought about the outside world. The immediate threat of survival was already overbearing enough to worry about what was happening ten miles down the road. I shot an awkward grin at Dalog to acknowledge his comment.

"See, check it. We're out here blowing holes in monsters, right? What's the White House doing? Is Obeezy out there clearing protocols to launch a strike? How deep does it go?" I shrugged.

"All I'm saying is, this can't be that under the rug. It'd be a hell of a lump under that rug if so," Dalog said, standing up from loading ammo,

"it's just too crazy. Oh, hey, bee tee dubs, I'm full up."

I poured one last box of ammo into the bag. I knew we were going to have regrets carrying all of this brass.

"Dude, we're like the guy in Doom or Wolfenstein who just rocks like a hundred guns and full ammo for each. This is gonna be tits," Dalog said as he stepped over boxes toward the door.

I waded through a sea of cardboard toward the door myself. We really did a number on this room. I felt at a few of my pouches on my vest, making sure I felt a full heavy magazine inside. I think we had more ammo this time than the last time we loaded up. X was going to shit herself with joy. She'd have more than enough ammo to avenge every single one of our friends and battle buddies. It was about to be a good day.

Dalog and I hooved it through the sands and gravel back to the barrier enclosure the remaining gang was at. Thankfully they were all still inside the enclave. X looked up at the two of us shuffling through the sand. You could hear us rattling from miles away I'm sure. We were full to bursting with enough ammunition to win three world wars.

"Jesus Christ. Where the hell were you two?" X snapped as she stood up from the ground.

I unslung the pack from my shoulder, letting it hit the ground with a clack. All of the magazines slamming into each other. "No shit," X started, "you guys went on an ammo run?" I nodded.

Dalog dropped his bag and unzipped the top, revealing his booty inside. He reached in for a standard magazine for the assault rifle and tossed one toward Whelan.

"Brother, you guys rock," Whelan said, inspecting the magazine.

We spent the next few moments loading up every pouch we had on our person. Pockets were filled. We were ready to rock and more or less also prepared to roll.

"Holy shit fucks. I was about to get everyone together and fan out for ya. Y'all didn't tell nobody where the hell ya went," Whelan said as he changed mags in his rifle.

"Yeah, our bad actually. I wandered off, and Chantry found this nice little ammo stash. It was the motherload," Dalog responded.

"Let me guess. Hidden secret level or some shit?" Whelan said sarcastically.

"May as well have been. That was tits to find."

"Mhmm," Whelan added to Dalog's statement.

I wasn't sure what the hell we were sitting around for. The gang had properly buried Martinez as best as one could in the hot weather. Thankfully it was still early morning, and the sun had started to breach the sky.

"Hey, crew. Let's get moving. We got a plane to catch," Rogers said as he stood to his feet using his rifle as a crutch.

He brushed the sand off him as he turned and walked toward the airfield. Whelan followed, not far tailed by Mr. Jarrett. I looked at X and Dalog, shrugged, and hurried along to catch up to Rogers and his massive powerwalking skills.

# Chapter 17

*FOB Centurion, IZ*
*0519 Local*
*February 14, 2010*

The airfield was in view after a fifteen-minute hike through the sands of Iraq. The base was that much quieter. I always thought the silence at night was peaceful, but now it's what sends chills down my spine. I didn't like the feeling one bit. Actually, I had this feeling a few times since this ordeal started. It's almost like Spider-Man when Goblin or something comes to get him. He had that sense about it. I had that. Maybe I'm Spider-Man? I better not let Dalog hear these thoughts. I'd be almost positive to think that he'd run with it and assume I have super strength or can fly or something.

Worse, he could think HE has powers.

While I drifted off into my fantasy of having powers, I lost track of everything. I was only snapped back into reality by my face slamming hard into Whelan's sweaty back.

"Stop, goddamnit," he whispered as he held his fist up to halt the team.

"Why? What?" I asked.

"Shh."

I stopped dead in my tracks. I heard it. At first, I thought I was imagining hearing something, but it was there. A low, soft rumble. It sounded like thunder clapping in the distance. A rolling thunder. The kind that booms, followed by a bunch of micro-booms to follow.

"The fuck?" X asked as she started walking forward toward the gate of the airfield.

There it was. In the distance, shrouded in a twilight haze of sunrise behind it. We could see everything. It was all there; airplanes, choppers, trucks. You name it, they were here. Except for the fact that they were on fire. That was the roaring sound we heard. The roar of open flames. The crackle of embers as they sparked away from the aircraft. We barely noticed the smoke due to it being dark. As we drew a little closer, the smoke was thick. It was apparent; something didn't want us to leave.

"Fuck! Fuck! Fucking shit ass ballbag!" Whelan yelled as he kicked sand and rocks from around him, punching the air in frustration.

I wanted to interject with something reassuring, but I had nothing.

"Bu-"

I was cut off by Rogers pointing wildly at something.

We all shifted our gaze to follow what he was flailing his arms at. There it was, in the backside of the airfield: a pristine, untouched chopper. I never could identify what the hell was what out here. A chopper was a chopper to me.

"Fucking A. She's a beaut," Whelan said as he slowly moved his feet toward the direction of the chopper.

A chopper is a chopper, and I stand by it. I think the only one I could pick out of a lineup was that one with the two blades. What was it? A Chinook? I think that's right. It looked different.

"Call Of Duty time!" Dalog yelled out as he caressed his rifle stock.

"An AH-64, gentlemen. Look at 'er. All American power. Named after the real American, the Apache. It's the sign that we're goin' home, ladies," Whelan said, almost reciting a speech from a movie I swear I'd seen during the deployment.

"You know how to fly that thing, right?" X asked, concerned for our wellbeing after surviving so much chaos.

Whelan looked at Rogers. Rogers gave a slight nod and a smile.

"I was born to do this," he bellowed as he picked up the pace down the small dirt hill that separated the airfield from the rest of the base.

I had to admit, there was a bit more pep in our step as we hiked toward the chopper. The heat didn't bother me, even though the flames were ripping around us from each direction. We skirted through the fire and ash on a mission. All around us was devastation. Someone, or something, didn't want us leaving this base. They made a mistake by leaving one chopper untouched. Something didn't sit right. It felt like bait.

"Guys, wait!" I cried out to the team.

Everyone came to a halt. I had to express the concerns I was having.

"It's a little convenient that one chopper is left standing, isn't it? Surrounded by flames at the far side of the airfield?" I expressed to the team.

Dalog shrugged. Mr. Jarrett didn't seem phased at all by what I just said.

"It *is* convenient. That's why we're takin' 'er," Whelan said.

"Yeah, man. Seize the carp!" Dalog added.

I shook my head. Was I the only one that was thinking logically? Did no one sense the danger we were headed into? I'm sure it was an ambush or rigged to explode.

"Listen. I think it's a trap. It's clearly bait for us," I explained.

"I know bait when I see it, Chantry. I'm a master baiter," Dalog chuckled, his bad joke not the least bit amusing to me right now.

Whelan smiled a bit. I think Dalog has finally grown on him.

Whatever it was, gave him pause to think.

"Sure. I hear ya. Let's get in there quietly and get the hell off this shithole," Whelan commanded to the team.

He squatted down a bit, facing the chopper.

"Ok, half and half. We're splitting up the middle, team A goes left, team B goes right. We are going to pincer that chopper. Something pops out of it, we'll be ready. Got it?"

I felt this plan was solid. It was better than mine was. My plan consisted of shitting myself, regrouping, and formulating a new plan. While I daydreamed about the plan, I barely noticed the team split up and start heading closer to the chopper. Weapons were drawn and ready to vaporize the first thing that leaped from the aircraft.

I opted to join the team with Whelan. He seemed like he had his shit together and something to live for. I didn't know much about Rogers. It's not that I didn't trust him, I just didn't get him. X and Mr. Jarrett followed him, while me and Dalog went with Whelan. I'm sure Whelan was pleased to know he'd be hearing a bunch of video game references while piloting the chopper.

The ground began to rumble under our feet. I could see the Apache in front of us, wiggling and shaking from the vibration. I whirled my head around to see what was happening. I was half expecting seeing half of the United States Army rolling through with tanks to handle business. I knew that wasn't the case. This was much, much worse.

"The fuck is that?" Dalog asked, shifting his helmet back to get a better view of the area.

I shrugged, clenching my rifle harder than ever. Whatever this was, it was big.

"Christ on a cross, look over there!" Whelan yelled, pointing to the corner of the terminal building.

The ground was raising and lifting. It was as if it was breathing. As if the earth was alive. This was not a good look for us.

I took a few steps backward, as did Whelan. In a burst of sand and Earth that resembled a Humpback whale breaching, something broke through the ground. There was so much sand floating through the air, it made it hard to see. I pulled my balaclava over my face to block the sand from getting into my lungs more than it already was. I needed the dust to settle. I could still hear rumbling. Whatever this was, it was big. It was so big, it was struggling to try to get out of the ground.

"Shit. It's a big-un," Whelan said as he stepped a few paces forward.

I could finally see it as the chaos settled a bit. Let me tell you, I'm not too scared of a lot of things. I'm not the first to jump into danger, but I'm also not afraid to face it head-on if need be. What I saw nearly made me turn tail and run back home and un-enlist. I wanted to just go home and play video games and watch TV and pretend I never did this whole dumb idea. This thing, from what I could see, resembled some type of giant arachnid. A goddamn spider or something. That isn't cool at all. I hate spiders. As the debris settled more, I could see the creature was trapped under some of the air terminal building debris. It bought us time to think and assess what the hell it was. A mutant Camel Spider from hell. I could see its tail, the legs, it's stupid spidery face. It was a cream color. The only thing I could say it looked like was a Camel Spider. They were terrifying enough at six inches big. Horrifying at a foot long. This thing made those look like an ordinary house spider.

As it emerged further from the sands, I could see it had two giant tails. One looked like it had a hook or spike on it. The other looked whip-like, almost like a prehensile tail an opossum would have from back home. The creature let out a roar. It sounded like a garbage truck grinding up its trash, combined with a dying elephant and the squeal of bad breaks. I could feel the bass of the roar in my chest. That's it. We're dead.

# Chapter 18

*FOB Centurion, IZ*
*0945 Local*
*February 14, 2010*

I couldn't believe my eyes. As the creature shook off the rest of the dirt from its body, I stared in disbelief. I was frozen in absolute and total horror.

"Fuck it. Balls deep!" Dalog yelled as he ran toward the creature. "Dalog!!!" the group screamed at him as he ran.

I watched as he ran toward the creature, firing a few rounds at it to draw attention.

He looked back at the group of us, "Start the chopper!"

We didn't hesitate. Whelan and Rogers sat in the cockpit and started assessing the situation. I watched as Dalog ran down the airfield toward this monster spider thing. He juked it a few times as he fired. I could see he changed magazines once as he drew nearer. It was enough to grab this things attention. It roared once more as it began to pursue Dalog.

Even though he was far enough away, I could see his expression change. He shifted direction as he started to run away from the creature.

He was leading it away. God bless that man, he was driving it away from us.

I watched as he disappeared over the hill, the sun blinding me as I stared. The creature dropped over the horizon, although it took much longer. It was calm. Too calm.

"Here they come!" X yelled out from behind me.

*I knew it.*

"Lock and load, fuckers! We got to get this thing off the ground. Buy me five minutes!" Whelan yelled from the chopper as he and Rogers fooled with switches.

I swiveled my head around and looked at what they meant. Everything. Everything was coming at us. Waves of Skitter Critters. Squadrons of Hellbugs were swarming in from above. I also saw some Big and Nastys positioning up on the hill in the distance. We were about to be hit by just about everything they had.

"I thought there were more than this," Mr. Jarrett said.

I turned around and shot him a look.

"The hell you mean, 'more than this?'" X shouted, "There ain't enough as it is?"

No one paid mind to his statement and began putting bullets into targets. X and I concentrated on the Hellbugs. Mr. Jarrett was taking out the Skitters as best as he could. I saw Whelan even left the chopper to help lay down some fire into the Skitters. They were dropping, but not fast enough.

I could hear engines priming and making noise as if they were trying to start some propellers. I didn't have the slightest clue how to be useful, other than killing everything in sight. X was ripping through these things with her 249, but it wasn't enough firepower. We needed bigger. I did my best to signal Weiland. I got his attention, and he started making his way toward me while shooting Skitters.

"Can we get one of the guns on a damaged ship to fire?" I asked.

"This ain't no dayum vid'ya game. But yeah. You learn that from your games?" Whelan asked.

I smiled. It's about time that Dalog and I had some useful knowledge from our games. He would have been proud to know I referenced a stupid game to save our asses. The two of us tried to shoot our way to the closest airship that was facing the direction of the chaos. I stood watch while he climbed into the cockpit. This was going to be amazing. I was about to be part of, and witness to, the greatest action movie moment in history.

I laid down more fire into the Skitters and put more rounds into the Hellbugs. We needed to hit the Big and Nasty crew, but our weapons wouldn't do much from down here. I watched as the team carefully skirted around the balls of energetic death, killing wave after wave of Skitter and Hellbug alike. Whelan worked diligently to get what was left of the system fired up. I really hoped he knew what he was doing.

"Get in!" He yelled from the half-blown out cockpit.

I climbed on board. Whelan was able to get what was left of the equipment powered up and running. Lights flickered on the console. Sparks emitted periodically from electronic parts that were foreign to me. He pointed to the turret that was fixed on the side of the door.

"Put holes in shit. You know how that works?" He asked.

I shrugged. "Pull the trigger, and things die, right?"
He smiled and nodded.

"Hang on! We're doing some next-level action movie shit!"

I had all of two seconds to grip a bar next to my head before he pulled on the stick. I realized what he was doing. We lurched off the ground, grinding our way to the left. We were violently but effectively rotating this hunk of smoldering metal to face the crowd of goons. It was amazing.

"Ok, grab this thing over here and make dead!" Whelan pointed to what I assumed were the weapon controls.

I sat down in the seat and assessed what I was doing. Some switches, knobs, and buttons all jumped out at me. Part of me wishes I could get on the internet and look this thing up. The other part of me was ready to squeeze whatever button was the trigger. I was interrupted from my action hero haze by a giant body brushing past me. Whelan reached over and pointed out the controls.

"The stick moves the gun. It's more fucked up than a football bat, so it ain't moving. You just need it to fire. See this red thing here? Flip that up and press the buttons under it. This other thing? Press that button too. Short bursts or you'll set our shit on fire," Whelan said, shifting back to his seat after his tutorial.

I did exactly as he said. Flipping switches, knobs, and buttons, I readied myself to be the bringer of death. Outside, I could see X and the rest of the crew firing at the crowd of uglies. Mr. Jarrett was using one of the extra pistols at this point, and doing an excellent job at it for a guy who never really held a gun or served before. His Eagles jersey getting covered in all sorts of rainbow colors of blood and guts as it sprayed his way.

Rogers was in a kneeling position, taking carefully aimed rifle shots, as compared to X blowing holes in everything to include the terrain, vehicles, and air with her 249. It was pandemonium gone wild outside. Even though the whirring engines, grinding gears, and other noises were loud, what was happening out there was louder tenfold.

I felt the chopper jerk once more to the left. I was almost lined up with one of the Big and Nasty's. I squeezed on the trigger. The sound was indescribable. The sound of that 30mm gun. The ole' Gatlin' Gun from those video games I played back in the 90s. The power behind it. The sound of it. It sounded like another set of propellers taking off, combined with a chainsaw. A chainsaw of absolute death. Six hundred-plus rounds firing out of this thing every minute. I wished I could count them to make sure, but I could feel the power and quantity.

I hadn't realized that my first six-second trigger squeeze eviscerated the first Nasty. It was cut in half, and its hands were ripped away from the upper body. I also saw part of one of the buildings behind it crumble a bit. This gun was legit.

"I got him! I got him! Suck it!" I yelled with joy.

"Don't get cocky, kid," Whelan said.

I'm not even sure he knows he made a Star Wars reference. Maybe he secretly liked this nerdy stuff too, hidden deep in his good ol' boy Texan exterior. The chopper bounced again, this time rocking over a bit. I could see we were sitting at an angle now, but not enough to bother me.

"I got maybe two more of those in me before the blades bury into the sand. Make it count!"

I nodded back to Whelan. I was almost lined up with the second Nasty. I decided to take a shot, maybe I could wing it with a stray bullet. I squeezed on the trigger. A grinding hum, as before, came ripping out of the front of the chopper. I was a human woodchipper. Come to think of it, maybe that's a better description of the sound. A woodchipper.

The second Nasty didn't react. It readied its stupid arm cannons once again to take another shot at the ground crew. I say ground crew as if I'm high up into the air doing aerial combat. As it charged up for its next shot, the right arm became separated, smashing down into the sand beside it. Victory is mine, stupid bug alien monster thing.

The arm was still charging. I'm assuming the blasters were charged at the fist, and not deep within the body somewhere. As the severed arm fired off, I don't think the Nasty counted on this being his last day. There's nothing more embarrassing than a cowboy shooting himself in the foot in a movie. What might be more embarrassing is having your laser-blasting arm shoot both of your tiny stump legs off your body from the ground.

The arm fired off an energy beam, cutting through the flesh of the Nasty. The remaining torso fell to the sand and began rolling down the hill. I chuckled at the sight. I was hoping Whelan saw how awesome this was.

We bounced the chopper once more. Thankfully we had enough parts together to pull this off. I spoke in my brain too soon. Once we skid into position, as we did a few times before, I heard it. A loud groan and crunch. The rear of the chopper snagged onto something big. I could hear it as it broke off the rear of the aircraft. The blades became tangled with the back half of the fuselage of the plane, chopping it off. The blades may have made it through, but not unscathed.

I took the opportunity and our new positioning to take a shot at the two Nasty's that were standing side by side. It was worth a chance for the hat trick. I squeezed the trigger. The woodchipper of the 30mm ripped through both of their bodies in a disgusting blue-green spray of death. Sherwin Williams probably doesn't even have paint in this shade.

"Nice. Let's get back to the others and kill these assholes," Whelan said as he gripped his rifle by the rails and jumped out of the cockpit.

I followed and got out on the other side. Big mistake. Once I landed and slung my rifle on myself once more, I looked around. The Camel Spider thing had come back around. Two thoughts crossed my mind; that of the fate of Dalog, and now mine. It towered me by at least two stories or so. I froze in place. I wanted to yell over to the group but couldn't find the means to do so.

"Hey, asshole! This is for Martinez!" X screamed out as she turned her machine gun onto the giant arachnid.

She continued to pump rounds into it as I stared like an idiot. I realized the monster was distracted and found my feet. I pushed myself away from the chopper and back to the group. I could see that X and Rogers were running low on ammunition. I could only imagine how many rounds they'd expended during this firefight.

I reached into my vest and tossed a mag to Rogers. Just in time, apparently, as his bolt slid back and locked.

"Whattaya, psychic buddy?" Rogers yelled as he dropped the empty mag to load the new one.

He used the new ammo to put holes in a handful of Skitters as they rounded the corner from the gate. I scanned around. No more Hellbugs, thank god. We just had a few Skitters and this one big giant spider thing. No biggie. I shuddered at the thought of the giant spider monster again. Even mutated and wild-looking, it was still a spider bug, and I got the willies.

I trained fire onto the giant arachnid. X looked over at me and smiled. She dropped her under-barrel belt feeder and reached into her bag for another. Thank god we packed a few of those from the arms room. I laid down distraction fire while she reloaded. I hated belt-fed weapons. I should say, I hated reloading them. I've seen what they can do, but they are a bitch to refill.

Mr. Jarrett stood alongside me as he fired his pistol at the Arachnid.

"Yo. We got a name for this asshole?" He asked.

I shrugged. Now was not the time to be thinking of clever names for the monsters. Big fucking spider bug thing should just about cover it at this point.

"Haven't given it much thought. You got anything?" I asked, changing out another magazine.

Mr. Jarrett smiled.

"Nah. But shoot its legs. That's gonna hurt it," He added.

Who the hell suggests a specific thing? It's not like it's a zombie and we are suggesting aiming for the head. Always try to aim for the head in a zombie apocalypse. I don't think we've ever had a movie about a giant bug monster with two tails that will likely kill us all. If there was, it must have been on the Sci-Fi channel on cable.

"The legs?" I asked.

"The legs," Jarrett added.

I fired my rifle at the legs. It squealed with pain but didn't seem too phased by what just happened. They were so skinny and hard to hit. X had just finished reloading her weapon and stood up to fire. I was about to yell to her to aim for the legs. I couldn't get the breath to escape my lungs. I also wanted to scream 'look out!'

The whip-like tail appendage flipped through and struck X in the torso, sending her flying across the airfield. I saw her crash land against some of the broken aircraft.

"Jesus Christ!" I screamed.

Rogers saw what happened and stepped into action. He began firing his rifle at the creature's face. Rogers didn't seem all too thrilled to see people that he probably just started getting to know, die in front of him. He began laying down fire with carefully controlled rounds. The only problem was that Rogers was shooting in the supposed strong points. He needed to go for the legs. The creature scuttled around on its legs, making it harder to aim for them. It was constantly repositioning. Smart little thing, ain't it?

"I'm gonna check on the girl!" Rogers yelled out, making his way over to X.

He shuffled his way over, as Whelan stepped in to lay down suppressive fire in his place.

"Legs, man. Legs." Jarrett said to Whelan.

His face must have contorted into the same confused expression I showed a few moments ago. He shrugged and refocused his attention on the arachnid beast.

As he fired, we noticed the stupid thing making its way toward X and Rogers. He was not going to finish the job. I decided to Rambo my way forward and distract it. I screamed what I thought was an intense battle cry and rushed forward. Whelan followed.

"I got this, kid. Go protect the Civi!" Whelan ordered as he continued my charge. I watched as the whip-like tail slammed into Rogers as he passed by the monster. He too was knocked for a loop, slamming against a concrete bunker piece.

"Fuck you, bug! I seen bigger bugs than you back home!" Whelan screamed as he opened fire on the creature.

He trained all of his rounds in the front right leg. It was working; the leg began to sever. The creature reared back and screamed its godawful battle cry once more. It was like nails on a chalkboard to me. Whelan didn't stop. Neither did I. We trained rounds into the next leg. It's fluids sputtering out of the wound we were making.

The second right leg began to come off. Once we could slow it down enough, it was much easier to hit. It began to peel away from the rest of the upper leg in a disgusting display of blood and other juices. I was focused on destroying this thing. The creature lost its balance and fell to the ground with a hard thud. It stopped fighting. It stopped moving.

Whelan didn't stop, however. He continued to move forward, putting rounds into the face of this thing. Honestly, the best idea any of us had. I've seen too many movies where the hero doesn't finish off the bad guy, and he gets up for one last hurrah. His rounds landed with precision. The creature wasn't moving. We won.

Whelan kept firing. He fired until the ever audible 'click' of the empty chamber. I heard him click a few times before stopping. Adrenaline and rage will do that to you, I suppose. He loosened his grip and let the rifle drop to his side. I looked at Mr. Jarrett.

"Good tip."

"Word," He responded.

I was seconds from rushing over to check on Rogers and X. I don't think the brainwaves made it to my feet as fast as I had hoped. Before I could do anything, I glanced back up at Whelan. He had turned around and started toward Rogers himself. I saw behind him, what seemed like slow motion. From the outside, it must have looked like a slowed-down scene in a movie. An explosion or crumbling building that should take a split second to happen. Hollywood instead seeing fit to drag it out for a minute or two. Maybe this is what it actually looks like in the moment?

The arachnid used its spikey scorpion-like tail. It whipped down with a crushing thud into Whelan, piercing his torso. Blood immediately shot out of his mouth as he looked down at the sharp spike protruding from his chest. He grabbed for his rifle, dropping the magazine. This son of a bitch was still going to fight? And I say that for both parties. Whelan fumbled for his magazine in his vest pouch, before slumping over in a cough filled sputtering of blood from his mouth.

"Goddamnit!!!" Screamed as I fired at the tail.

The arachnid stood back up on its remaining legs. I now stood alone. I've felt alone before. Hell, I've felt alone during this whole ordeal before. I think this was a worse feeling than any of those times previously.

Mr. Jarrett worked to train his pistol on the creature. He was not back up by any means. X and Rogers were laid out just a few meters from me. We were screwed in every sense of the word. I decided to make peace with the world I was in and prepare for the next chapter.

# Chapter 19

*FOB Centurion, IZ*
*1300 Local*
*February 14, 2010*

I decided to close my eyes. I'd rather not see what obliterates me. My heart raced. I could feel sweat running down my face. Or were those tears? I couldn't tell you. I didn't even worry about what Mr. Jarrett was doing. I could hear him still wasting 9mm ammunition by firing at this thing. Is this how I die? I always pictured my death differently. I figured I'd be a little older. Maybe have a family or something. I just thought it'd be something stupid like a car accident. Or perhaps the amount of bacon I eat ends up stopping my heart. I wasn't going to die like this.

I mustered up whatever fortitude I had in my body. I rallied my cojones to fight back. I opened my eyes and wiped my face off. Readying my rifle, I began to squeeze rounds off into the legs once more. As I squeezed the trigger, my rifle sounded very different. It almost sounded like a woodchipper. I watched as the legs of this thing ripped away from its body. The tails were torn apart. The carapace of its terrifying brown-ish grey body was pierced as it fell to the sand once more.

"What the shit?" I yelled out.

I glanced over to my side. Dalog was in the gunner's seat of the

Apache. He was squeezing wildly at the triggers, activating the giant gun of death that was housed under the cockpit. I'd never been happier to see anyone in my life. I guess he just kept running and survived.

The creature yelled out a few more howls in its death throes. It flailed what was left of its nubby legs. I didn't hear the gun stop. He continued to fire into it. Even though most of the rounds were annihilating the sand, he didn't stop. Between him and I, we pissed through over a thousand rounds. I heard the barrel spinning, but nothing more followed. He eased off the trigger, allowing the whirring barrel to come to a halt. It was quiet. The quietest I've heard this place in a long time. Even with the rippling flames, it was silent.

I looked around. There wasn't anything in sight. It was still. I didn't know if I should check with Dalog or check with X and Rogers. I opted for the guy I could talk to. At least he could help me triage the injured. I walked over to the cockpit door and helped him out. The chopper was practically sideways at this point.

"Holy fuck, man. That was one of the coolest things I've been able to do in my life. I'd rather it be under better circumstances though," Dalog joked as he stood to his feet after jumping to the ground.

I had questions. A lot of them. I wanted to calmly ask them in an orderly fashion, but my adrenaline was pumping too hard to rationally say or do anything.

"How the hell do you know how to use this thing?" I asked, starting to walk toward X and Rogers.

"Umm. Well, see, there's this thing called video games. And I play them. It wasn't that hard to sort out, really."

I shook my head at him. Who knew that video game knowledge was that useful?

"Everyone ok? What did I miss?" Dalog asked.

My expression changed. Dalog knew something was wrong and began to look around. He saw I was heading toward X and Rogers. Mr. Jarrett found himself resting against a broken barricade, smoking a Black and Mild cigar. I focused my attention on what remained of Whelan. I didn't even know if that was a first name or the last name. I didn't know his family, or where he lived. It dawned on me I knew nothing about this guy.

"Fuck, man. That guy was a dickbag, but he didn't deserve that. What happened?" Dalog asked, shifting his attention back to me.

"Sacrificed himself before you got here. It honestly may have been what saved us. A few seconds later, you would have been coming back to an empty lot."

"Mhmm," Dalog added.

We crunched through debris and sand up to where X and Rogers were laying. They were not far from each other, thankfully. We made it to Rogers. I knelt down to check on him. He was still breathing. That was a relief. Dalog poked him with the toe of his boot. Rogers began to cough. A sign that he was still with us.

"Christ, buddy. You ok?" I asked, shifting over closer to his face.

He wheezed a bit before moving his eyelids open. His eyes darted around, trying to take in the surroundings.

"What happened? Did we win?" He muttered.

I nodded.

"Yeah, the big thing is dead. The little things are dead. We did ok, overall."

He tried to sit up. Dalog and I did our best to sit him upright. I shot a glance at Mr. Jarrett, who took the hint. He sauntered over to help us. He rested against a bit of fence and continued to smoke.

Dalog went to check on X, who was already starting to stand on her own. You could tell she was knocked for a loop. She staggered and stumbled to her feet.

"The good chopper. Was it untouched?" Rogers gasped out.

I looked over my shoulder. It stood in the distance, completely untouched. I have to admit, it was shocking to see. I figured it would be mangled into a thousand pieces by the creatures.

"Yeah, we're good man," I said back to Rogers.

He smiled and laid his head back down. He was hurt pretty bad but seemed like he'd make it. X stumbled over with the help of Dalog to our location.

"Got it?" She asked.

I figured I'd be telling the same story once again.

"Yeah. Do you see a giant spider monster from hell trying to eat us? We're good."

I didn't realize I was still keyed up from the adrenaline and sounded snarky. We were going around in circles by sitting here doing nothing but telling the same story.

"Whelan?" Rogers asked, starting to try to sit up.

"He, he was brave. He did what I didn't think I could do. He faced that asshole head-on and was a damn hero," I said.

He laughed with a muffled cough.

"That asshole. Whelan always wanted to be a war hero. Close enough, I guess. His wife is going to be pissed at 'im."

I don't know what kind of bond these guys had with each other. I'm assuming that the humor was what held some people together. If you really sat and thought about it, the situation was unfortunate. Making a joke might be the best way to cope at this moment.

"Help me to that hunk of metal, and we will fly far from this shithole," Rogers continued, "I'm ready to go."

Dalog and I helped Rogers to his feet. Mr. Jarrett aided X, and the group of us shuffled over to the helicopter. We were getting off this butthole of a base.

Rogers was dumped into the pilot seat. He groggily began hitting switches. The engine whirred to life. The beautiful hum of freedom rang in my ears. We all buckled in. The propeller blade began to spin. This was happening. I could barely contain my excitement and relief as we felt the pull of the blades lift us from the ground. Mr. Jarrett sat up front, riding shotgun next to Rogers. It was better that way, leaving us with the guns to take out whatever came our way.

I looked outside of the aircraft. I watched as the base that I lived at, my home for six or seven months, grew smaller and smaller. It was eerie. Not one person walking around. No vehicles driving. There was absolutely nothing going on. I'd been in aircraft before and watched out the windows at the hustle and bustle of the base. Polar opposite. Rogers began to tilt us forward, headed to some base that he and Mr. Jarrett discussed might have the best chance for survivors.

We floated along above the base. There was no worry about being shot at, rocketed, or any of the usual airborne drama we would receive; everyone was dead. Or, at least, the next best thing. I hoped that whatever was going on, we could cure the lot of survivors we saw underground. All of those civilians, soldiers. Eriks. Everything was just insane.

I looked over at X. She was really out of it from being cracked in the guts by the Scorpion King. Hell, now that I think about it, that's a solid name. That whole ordeal was a disaster, much like that movie that came out not too long ago. I think that was around when I was in high school. They did The Rock dirty in that one. That's what I'll call this thing until we figure something out; Scorpion King. It looked half scorpion, half camel spider, so fuck it.

X caught me looking at her.

"You ok?" She asked as she sat up from slouching in the seat.

Yeah. Just thinking, that's all," I responded, trying to seem nonchalant about being busted staring at people.

"I feel like at any moment, I'm going to wake up, and be back in my office. Like this was all a bad dream," X said.

"Well, we survived, and the monster is dead," I said doing my best to reassure that we were still ahead in points.

"True. I'm shocked Dalog came through. I thought he was dead. I can't lose anyone else. Heck, I'm shocked you even got this far."

"Gee, thanks. Glad to know I'm a regular Rambo in your book." X leaned forward.

"Nah, it's just you never really seemed like a fighter. You kicked ass out there. Sergeant Matthews would be proud that you weren't some lazy soldier who just played video games with Dalog."

I thought about that for a second. These people were all dead. There wasn't anything that could be done about it. Our command staff. Superior officers. Co-workers. Fellow soldiers. Our brothers and sisters. These people were gone. Far as we could tell, we were all we had left. We might just be the only ones left in the world, as unlikely as that sounds.

"Well, if it's any consolation, Happy Valentine's Day," I joked.

X smiled for a second.

"Barking up the wrong tree, dirtbag," she laughed as she sat back to look out of the side window.

I panned around the interior one last time. Rogers and Mr. Jarrett had headsets on, chatting it up with each other about where to go. Dalog was racked out, a well-deserved nap. We were alive, and we were safe. I didn't even care where we were headed. I rested my helmet against the chopper and closed my eyes. In seconds, I was asleep.

# Chapter 20

*Unknown*
*1700 Local*
*February 14, 2010*

I was awoken by a ton of noise and action. The chopper was shaking and moving wildly. We were still in the air. The Apache did its best to dodge rockets and rounds as we sailed through the air. Part of me was relieved to be getting shot at once more. It meant they weren't the bug monsters from Mars. It meant there was still a shred of friggin' hope.

I decided to reach over and grab the headset.

"Where we at? What's up?" I asked over the radio.

Mr. Jarrett turned around to make eye contact with me. "Getting shot at. We about five minutes from hitting Joint Base Python. We went south," he said, shifting back to face front.

Python? I'd never been there. I heard it's a decent base. They have a pool, among other luxuries. This should be nice. So long as we don't die on the way in. I can't have made it this far only to be a smear on the tarmac after a crap landing. The chopper bobbed and wove through the various rounds and descended at an alarming speed. It was more than enough to wake up the snoozing Dalog.

"Yo, what? Wait? Where?" He said, panicked as he gained awareness of his surroundings.

"We're over Python. Getting shot at," I assured him.

"Oh, well, that's good then."

Dalog closed his eyes and attempted to go back to sleep.

The ride over the base was a long one. We dove in, dropping several hundred feet. We were flying much lower than I was comfortable with. There was a bit of a sandstorm out, so it was hard to see if everyone was a monster or just the typical asshole.

The chopper touched down at what I could assume was an airbase. I readied my rifle, ready for whatever breed of beastie they had on this dump.

"Hey, we're here, kiddos," Rogers called over the headset.

Situation normal? Was it all ok? Well, that was a hell of a relief. I can't wait to get someone with some brass on their chest to make a call to turn Centurion into a glass parking lot. Maybe they can build a Wal-Mart there. I loosened my grip on the rifle. The chopper door slid open. Someone on the outside was deboarding us. I felt like a VIP and wondered where my red carpet was.

"Step out of the chopper please," a mysterious voice called to us through the dust cloud.

The chopper blades whirred down to a stop. It was so much quieter without the constant whapping sound of the blades. Heck, we may have attributed to most of the dust cloud I couldn't see through.

Dalog cracked his neck and climbed toward the door. X followed him shortly after. I procrastinated, taking my sweet time crawling out. I was grabbed by my vest straps and hurried along.

"Hey, hey! Easy with all that," I cried out to the unknown manhandler.

Jarrett and Rogers both joined us on the side of the chopper. I could make out the figures as the other soldiers came into view. They were just that; soldiers. I was happy to see people. I was more delighted to see armed people. The upside is that they were friendly soldiers. The downside, however, is that all of their weapons were trained on us.

The guy to my right started to grab for my rifle. I reached for his hand and stopped him. Every rifle trained on me immediately. I heard the clatter of the carbon. The flicking of the safety switch. I was about to be full of holes. I let go and put my hands up.

Rogers came over and joined us in the kneeling position we were being forced into. Mr. Jarrett sauntered over and took a knee as well. What the hell was going on? Do they not know about what is going on out there? We really didn't have time for this.

A large, hefty gentleman in a brown suit began walking in our direction. I couldn't distinguish his face since the sun was just perfectly in my way. He was joined by someone in Army ACU uniform. He seemed older, maybe high ranking. Just the guy I need to talk to. I need answers. I wanted them to send support. I wanted a soda. I had a lot of demands.

"Mr. Jarrett. A pleasure to see you again so soon. Friends of yours?" The suited man asked.

"Word," Mr. Jarrett responded.

The man looked over to his soldiers. They instantly let us go and helped us to our feet. I now had more questions. I still needed that Coke. Maybe we can escalate that to the stupid energy drinks we have out here. I could go for a Rip-It at this point.

"Was everything ok? You shouldn't be here," The suited man asked.

"Well, Bronson, we'd be ok if you didn't have some garbage ass security detail up there," Jarrett responded.

*Garbage ass detail? What are they talking about? The incident? The monsters? Bronson?*

"We understand that there were some failsafe's that, well, failed. My team has been working on that."

"Failsafe's that almost got my ass ate!" Jarrett barked back at Bronson.

Dalog dusted his pants off and stepped forward, getting everyone's attention.

"Look. I just came from a base where I was literally shitting my pants every second. I was running from monsters, demons, aliens, or whatever the fuck you want to label them for the past three or four days. I want to know what's happening!" Dalog said, getting into Bronson's personal bubble.

"In time, soldier," Bronson responded in his grave, mysterious sounding voice.

I couldn't quite place where Bronson was from. He reminded me of Kingpin from the Spider-Man cartoons in the 90s. He had a Candyman-esque deep voice. He was clearly a villain. Maybe he was a good guy, but he gave me villain vibes. I was ready to see his secret lair hidden in a volcano at this point.

The older soldier figure stepped forward.

"Casualties?" he asked.

"Too many to count, sir," Jarrett responded.

"Christ. I should have dusted that site when we first discovered it." Bronson got visibly upset.

"Dusted it? This could make us a fortune! We could be gods!" He snarled at the older soldier.

The older gentleman wasn't having his attitude much longer.

"Don't forget who gave you the clearance to begin the dig!" He barked back.

Bronson recoiled a bit. The older soldier stepped to the side, allowing me to see him a bit better from where I was. Stellars. Colonel type. He was much older than anyone out here with us. He had seen some things. He had a few pins and patches that showed he had done some hardcore stuff in his past. He had his wings, which meant he did a lot of time in planes. He had an infantry badge, which said he probably did some hardcore shit. I didn't want to cross him, personally.

"Colonel Stellars? Mind if I say something?" Jarrett asked.

Stellars seemed visibly gruff but gentle at the same time. I felt like he may be the kind of leader who is approachable but gets stuff done. He looked a bit like that one guy, what was his name? Sam Elliot? Old dude with the thick mustache. I couldn't confirm that this guy wasn't Sam Elliot, but he could have been his twin.

"Well, after my initial report, things went belly up. I lost coms with everyone, then it was all over. The fan hit the shit," Jarrett said to

Stellars.

Stellars grunted with frustration.

"Goddamnit. Get everyone into the bunker. We got to sort this whole thing out."

I was pushed along by a soldier behind me. The group of us began to walk toward a giant metal building just outside of the airfield. Everything was so calm and normal. Does anyone know how bad it is up there?

We approached the giant metal building. A large door creaked open, and the sound of some mechanical noises followed from behind it.

Inside, a massive lift was waiting for us. I called it. Evil lair.

"Is no one bothered by what is going on at all?" X said, finally speaking up after being silent for so long.

I nodded but said nothing.

We boarded the lift. It was a huge mechanical industrial style lift. I assume based on its size, it should be hauling giant trucks and military equipment. Bronson pressed the large red button on the lift door. The platform groaned and creaked, and we began to decent.

# Chapter 21

*Joint Base Python, IZ*
*1900 Local*
*February 14, 2010*

We crept lower and lower. It was almost as low as we went when we were creeping down that mine. Hundreds of feet of rock wall and dirt went by. The frame of the shaft was supported by some man-made beams of steel. There were lights every so many feet, which helped me keep count of the depth. I had no idea how far we actually were, however.

"Almost there," Bronson assured.

"Great. Can we stop by the Orange Julius when we get to the bottom?

Is there a merry go round here as well?" Dalog asked, trying to be funny.

Bronson was not amused. He averted his gaze from Dalog and looked forward once more.

"Are all evil elevators that lead to a bad guy lair this long?" I asked Dalog.

He chuckled at the thought. I guess it was reassuring to know that he wasn't alone with his worries.

The lift crunched into the dirt below and stopped with a loud bang. The gate slowly opened, giving way to a long metallic hallway that leads to various doors and rooms. People in uniform, suits, and lab coats peppered the area. There was a lot of hustle and bustle down here for being the core of the Earth.

The air was surprisingly cool, clean, and refreshing. This was the better of my underground experiences this week. I would not recommend the last stay, a one-star review on Yelp.

"Stick with me. Do not touch anything. Do not look at anything. Do not talk to anyone," Bronson said.

We started to walk down the long, white and blue corridor. It was lined with some fancy lights, maybe LED. Against instructions, I peeked into the various rooms we passed by. I saw board rooms, offices and meeting places. Nothing eventful. Why the hell couldn't this stuff be on the surface?

"Keep close. We are going to the left," Bronson said.

I passed by even more offices through the hallways. I was catching the various names of the people. Some had military rank. Some were doctors. One grabbed my attention: S. Jarrett. That had to be this guy. They had to be the same. I also thought Jarrett was his first name, but I never saw a badge or an ID. I wonder what the S stood for? It bugged me as we rounded the final corner, stopping in front of two giant metal blast doors.

"Give me a moment. Prepare yourselves," Bronson said.

The old Colonel said nothing. He kept his military bearing the entire time, making this situation even more uncomfortable. I decided to up the ante on the comfort levels.

"So, S. Jarrett, care to tell us what you do here?" I asked coyly.

He shot a glance over at me. He knew I knew he worked here. That confirms that it was his name on the door of that office.

"Oh, uh-" Jarrett began, before the doors interrupted him.

The blast door clicked and clacked as it raised up. It seemed like it was held in place by robust locks or gears. I don't know how these things work. I never entered an evil lair before. I shot a glance over to

Dalog, who was staring at what lies beyond the doors. I turned my attention back.

"Shitballs," I whispered under my breath.

"Ditto," Dalog said.

"Fucksticks," X said.

The door clicked and locked in place above our heads.

"Word," Jarrett said.

Beyond the threshold, we saw hundreds of computers, scientists, and more. It was like that scene from Independence Day where they see Area 51 for the first time. This was surreal.

We each stepped inside, the door closing behind us once all of us were through. I turned and looked to watch the door close. Once it shut, I resumed my stares. The whole team stared. I was filled with a billion emotions. Those of anger, fear, anxiety, and at least ten more that I couldn't identify.

Before us lies a giant hangar-like building. Cages and containment systems filled the room, as well as exam tables. Housed in these were Skitters, Big and Nasty, and the Hellbug. Everything we had battled, just sitting here in cages. There were things I hadn't seen before. They were making them? They were breeding them? I needed to know.

"What the absolute fuck are you doing with all of these?" I screamed.

The entire room stopped working.

"Allow me to explain everything to your team once we meet up with my colleague. Trust me," Bronson said as he motioned to a female scientist across the room.

She walked over to us in a sultry walk. For being a scientist, she wore high heels. She had long dark brown hair. Her features were soft. She was kind of hot for a scientist. Then again, I'm not sure if there's a requirement for how a scientist is supposed to look.

"Everyone, this is Doctor Kowolski. She is head of the research team of the Terranisms," Bronson said.

"Terranisms?" X asked.

"Yes. Terranisms. They are organisms that are Earth borne by design," Kowolski said.

We each looked at each other in disbelief.

"You mean they were already here? Or did you all mix them with some shit you found outside?" Dalog questioned, getting visibly upset with Doctor Kowolski.

She smiled.

"Let's get you some rest. We have quarters set up for you. Let's talk about this all in the morning," Kowolski said, motioning to her assistant.

I had a billion and one questions. I mulled them over as we walked down a hallway and were key carded through a door to some living area. There were rooms with beds and all of the necessities. The soldiers escorting us pointed us into designated rooms. The door closed behind me as I entered. A prisoner in an evil lair, great.

Inside my room was a shower, radio, television, and a primo bed. Much nicer than the accommodations on my old base. I immediately gave up any care of my imprisonment and hit the shower. It had been days since I rinsed off. I was ready to get the stink of the day off my body.

The water was hot. Hotter than the base could even provide. It was a private shower, so it was nice to not look at strange wang flapping around because people can't wrap towels around their waist. I zoned out as the water hit my body. I barely noticed the twenty pounds of dirt coming off me, spiraling down the drain.

I exited the shower and dried off with a towel. I rummaged through the closet these mystery soldiers provided because I'll be damned if I put on the stank nasty clothing after all that. I felt amazing. Inside the closet were sweatpants, basic gray and white shirts, and slippers. I threw those onto my body, along with some generic underwear they left for me. They fit well, for not knowing I was coming. Somehow they knew a guy who wears a size 32 waist was going to be here? Or did they know more than they let on?

I tried the door in a futile attempt to discover what I already knew. Locked. I shuffled over in my slippers and sat on the bed. I turned on the radio, letting it play whatever was already on. It was preprogrammed music, which I assume is because no radio signal was making it down here. Some soft Jazz music played. I laid my head against the pillow. The pillow felt amazing. This was heaven but trapped in hell. Before I realized it, my body gave out. I passed out from everything. Between exhaustion, excitement, and this godly pillow, it took me. I drifted off into my dreams, far from this chaos.

*The monster invasion was tomorrow's problem...*

# About the Author

Harry Carpenter, Born 1985, in Baltimore, Maryland. By the age of 26, he had experienced plenty of things in his life through various employment, his first marriage, and a plethora of other situations in his life. His first book, "Tales From an Ex-Husband," recounts experiences with his first wife. His writing spans comedy to horror, as an avid fan of both. He likes cats.

# Also by Harry Carpenter

Tales From An Ex-Husband
Spooky Tales and Scary Things
Brain Dump

Made in the USA
Middletown, DE
08 January 2020